"You're not my friend."

Scorn laced five-year-old Amy's voice.

"I'd like to be," Clayton said calmly.

She bit her lip, her eyes narrowing.

Clay felt totally mystified by this small bundle of femininity. She was laughing one moment and bristling with fury the next. What did he know about dealing with any of that?

And yet, if he got the chance to marry Maryann, Amy would become his daughter....

"I hate you!" Amy spat out the words.

Clay just widened his eyes. "Really? I'm sorry about that. Maybe another time we can be friends, then." And he turned and walked away, leaving Amy to stomp her little foot in frustration.

"Ooh!" she fumed. "You don't know anything!"

Books by Lois Richer

Love Inspired

A Will and a Wedding #8
†*Faithfully Yours* #15
†*A Hopeful Heart* #23
†*Sweet Charity* #32
A Home, a Heart, a Husband #50
This Child of Mine #59
*Baby on the Way #73
*Daddy on the Way #79

†Faith, Hope & Charity
*Brides of the Seasons

LOIS RICHER

credits her love of writing to a childhood spent in a Sunday school where the King James version of the Bible was taught. The majesty and clarity of the language in the Old Testament stories allowed her to create pictures in her own mind while growing up in a tiny Canadian prairie village where everyone strove to make ends meet. During her school years, she continued to find great solace in those words and in the church family that supported her in local speech festivals, Christmas concerts and little theater productions. Later, in college, her ability with language stood her in good stead as she majored in linguistics, studied the work of William Shakespeare and participated in a small drama group.

Today Lois lives in another tiny Canadian town with her husband, Barry, and two very vocal sons. And still her belief in a strong, vibrant God who cares more than we know dominates her life. "My writing," she says, "allows me to express just a few of the words God sends bubbling around in my brain. If I convey some of the wonder and amazement I feel when I think of God and His love, I've used my words to good effect."

Daddy on the Way
Lois Richer

Published by Steeple Hill Books™

STEEPLE HILL BOOKS

ISBN 0-373-87079-5

DADDY ON THE WAY

Visit us at www.steeplehill.com

Printed in U.S.A.

Dear children, let us not love with words or tongue,
but with actions and in truth.

—*I John* 3:18

To my friend Andrea,
who critiques so gently and yet so well.

Thanks, friend.

Chapter One

"Ms. MacGregor, could you please tell us if your husband's alleged relationship with Miss Constein really happened?"

"They don't make any bones about baring their fangs, do they?" Clayton Matthews grimaced as the reporters flocked around the tall, slim woman who was just climbing out of her car. He leaned against the edge of his truck, watching the three-ring circus that had somehow taken over Oakburn, Minnesota.

"That kind never do." His friend Jordan Andrews shifted the grocery sack from one hip to the other and frowned. "Maryann looks as if she can handle it, though."

Clay searched the familiar face, looking for some telltale sign that Maryann was bothered by the indictment. But despite the flurry of reporters and their unending questions, he saw nothing on that beautiful frozen mask that hinted at her inner feelings. He peered at her. It had been months since she'd left and according to the reporters, she still used her own name.

"I have no comment. Please, let me pass." Maryann kept her face inscrutable, her head upright and her shoulders back as she picked her way through the hoard of reporters plaguing her every step.

"Maybe I should go help her out?" Clay asked his friend.

Jordan wrapped his hand around Clay's arm, stopping the other man's sudden rush forward. He shook his head. "I don't think that's a good idea, Clay. It will only make them ask more questions, speculate more. Besides, she looks like she's doing fine."

"Does Miss Constein's lawsuit against your husband's assets have some foundation?"

"Nosy Parkers!" Their rudeness got Clay's dander ruffled. "Don't these people have any inhibitions?"

"Reporters?" Jordan snorted. "Come on, Clay. They're after the story. And Maryann is big news right now. Especially with that woman's lawsuit."

Clay fumed as he watched the bloodhounds of journalism, each one out-yelling the other in hopes of eliciting a usable quote.

They'd descended on Maryann's former home in Oakburn like a swarm of hungry locusts after honey, and yet she ignored them as if they were no more than pesky mosquitoes. Clay figured it was an art she'd obviously learned in her years away from home. Personally, he'd never perfected it. He bristled indignantly as a reporter pushed a microphone into her face.

"Surely you know whether or not your husband ever had an affair with this woman?" A snide look curled the reporter's lips.

Clay clenched his fists, flinching as Maryann's face momentarily blanched even whiter than its normal parchment color. Her beautiful eyes grew dark and impenetrable in the flash of pain that he caught just before her lashes fell, hiding whatever she was feeling deep inside.

"I have no comment."

"I'd like to put an end to this right now." Clay was aghast. "How dare they insinuate such a thing?"

"They'll dare that and a lot more," Jordan muttered. "And it doesn't look like they're giving up anytime soon. Look at all those cameras."

"If it was me, my stomach would be tied in fifty knots." Clay studied Maryann's body language for some sign of distress, but the widow didn't seem fazed.

Instead, she sauntered regally forward, ignoring the chaos around her as if it mattered not a whit. Of course, this coolly elegant woman wasn't the shy, soft-spoken Maryann that Clay remembered from his youth. Smooth, polished and classy, she bore no resemblance to the needy young girl he'd known ten years ago.

This woman was probably used to a media feeding frenzy.

"If it was you, they wouldn't be asking any questions." Jordan laughed. "You lead a dull, boring life, Clayton." He winked at his friend. "A beautiful woman, on the other hand, always enhances the fiction they like to create." Jordan straightened, his mouth tightening, as a reporter placed a hand on Maryann's arm, halting her progress, his foot firmly planted in the blooming tulips that grew along the fence.

"One more like that guy and we move in," Clay said gritting his teeth.

"Aw, come on, Ms. MacGregor!" The reporter pressed closer. "Give us something."

"I have no comment." Maryann carefully side-stepped the man and continued on her way.

Clay watched the reporters follow her, then move directly into her path, surrounding her as she opened the gate that led to Wintergreen, the old Victorian home in which she'd chosen to hide herself. It was here she'd come to escape these horrible probing demands. It was here she'd chosen to stay, her closest friends nearby to offer support.

The awful things they were saying made Clay wince. She'd kept her troubled past hidden from the townspeople for as long as she could, protected Oakburn from the slanderous words and nasty rumors about one of their own.

But the gossips had followed her back, bringing their demeaning innuendos and personal indictments to the place she now shared with Caitlin and Beth, her two high school friends. Yet, she still hadn't confided in anyone—not even him. Clay could remember a time when she'd told him everything. He had been her best friend.

At least he thought he'd been.

"Ms. MacGregor, did your daughter know of your husband's—"

"That's enough." Clay straightened, his mouth tight. "You try and stop them, Jordan, I'll get her inside."

"Okay. Go." Jordan bounded forward like a St. Bernard, ready to protect.

"Excuse me." Clayton pushed his way forward and grasped Maryann's arm, elbowing the rudest of her pursuers out of her way. It wasn't much, but getting her through this maze was the least he could do for an old friend.

"Hey, we're holding a news conference here, buddy. The wife who was left out in the cold—"

Clay deliberately cut him off and offered a cocky response. "Didn't you hear, *buddy?* Ms. MacGregor has no comment. Not today, not tomorrow, not next week. Her husband is dead. Anything he may or may not have done is between him and God now. Could we leave it that way? Please?"

Clayton squeezed her hand with his fingers as he drew Maryann through the throng, along the sidewalk and up the stairs.

"Just keep going," he whispered, smiling into her huge dark eyes. "Jordan's right behind. We're almost there."

"Are you the new man in Ms. MacGregor's life, sir?" A woman Clayton had never met bellowed the question inches from his left ear, her voice implying that he was merely the latest in a long line.

"No, ma'am! I'm the old one," Clayton snapped back angrily, and then slammed the door in their faces.

"What a rude bunch." Vaguely he could hear Jordan outside, ordering them off the property, but Clay's attention was focused on Maryann.

Why hadn't she alerted the police to this mob, told her housemates to expect these dirt-diggers and their shabby suggestions? She could have asked *him* for help.

But then Maryann didn't confide in him anymore. And she'd always been reserved, worried about what people would think. Maybe she was uncomfortable repeating the scandalmongers' ugly hearsay to her friends.

And that's all it was, of course. No one in his right mind would cheat on Maryann MacGregor!

"I don't know how you can stand it," he said to her.

Maryann shrugged out of her daffodil-yellow lamb's wool jacket. "They're aggressive, but they aren't nearly as bad as some in the city," she murmured, her head bent to avoid his searching eyes. "I've learned to deal with it."

"Why should anyone have to deal with that? It's an invasion of privacy." He frowned as the door pushed open. In one twist of his body, he managed to shield her from the explosion of flashbulbs.

"Way to go, Clay. Now keep moving while I do a little negotiation, will you?" Jordan winked, easing inside the hall and shoving the door closed behind himself. It was clear from the lunge of bodies that the reporters weren't letting up. "Think I'll call the sheriff for backup."

Clayton nodded and with one hand on her back, guided Maryann up the curving staircase of the regal old mansion that had lately been divided into three apartments. His lips tightened with disgust at the callous treatment of this shy, quiet woman. No matter how well she'd handled them, the Maryann he knew hadn't really changed. He'd seen her vulnerability before she left town three months ago. He could still see it.

"How dare they come into town and start asking people these things? As if anyone believes that bunch of garbage! I don't know who buys those gossip papers. They're too unreal to be true."

Maryann swallowed, forcing the words down.

He doesn't know anything. Just keep up the facade. Her brain issued the orders automatically. *Clay's a friend. Besides, everything will be fine. It will all get better.*

She almost laughed. It wouldn't get better, of course. That was just another of the lies she told herself to keep herself focused on getting through one more day.

"I suppose they feel they have the right to speculate about us. After all, Terrence was a very high-profile public figure," she said, slipping her key inside the lock and opening the door with a sigh of relief. Home, at last! Once Clayton left, she could relax and quit pretending her mixed-up life was nearly perfect.

And Clayton would leave soon. He had to. The reporters would chew up a nice guy like him without a qualm. Besides, Maryann didn't want him hanging around, probing into her feelings, past or future. There was no room for a nice guy like Clay in her life. Not anymore.

The reporters and their ability to trail her were one of the reasons she'd chosen this upstairs apartment at Wintergreen when her old high school friends had insisted she move in with them.

The living area overlooked the huge garden space behind the Victorian monstrosity. Beyond the garden, a private reserve covered with thick trees, prickly wild rosebushes and an electric fence ensured no one could spy on her without being detected.

"I like what you've done with the place."

Maryann flinched at his words, surprised that she'd forgotten he was still there. That was going to be the problem with Clayton. He could slide back into her life so easily, and she could lean on him without even trying. She couldn't let that happen. Above all else, she had to avoid him as much as possible before he found out her secret.

"I'm glad you like it. It suits me, though there's a long way to go yet."

Clayton stood waiting by the door, gazing around the bright, sunlit room with a soft, yearning look on his face. He took in every detail of the rich royal-blue carpet, the sparse furniture and the sheer white organdy curtains where they billowed from the spring breeze blowing in the window. She saw his perusal stop when it came to the gigantic mural she'd painted across the facing wall.

"This looks like Addie's Glen," he murmured, peering at the sparkling water with lily pads dotting the surface, the thick green fern fronds waving in the wind, and the brilliant blue sky.

"It is. I painted it from memory last winter. Caitlin told me the Glen's gone now. Bulldozed to make room for more low-cost housing, I think she said. What a shame." Maryann couldn't explain how sad that made her. The single most important place in her life had been wiped out.

"I didn't think you'd remember."

She twisted around to gauge his expression. What did he mean? Did he think she'd shaken off the memories as easily as she'd left him and this place behind ten years ago? Did she wear her mask so well that even Clayton suspected her of becoming what she appeared to be?

"Of course I remember it. Addie's Glen was where I learned enough geometry to pass my junior year." She smiled, harking back to those difficult school years and Clayton's easy handling of them. "You were a good tutor."

Clay had changed since Jordan and Caitlin's wedding last Christmas. He seemed less nervous around her, less worried about impressing her. Maryann couldn't help wondering if that was a good thing. She didn't want him to be too friendly.

"You were a good student."

Maryann had to look away from the bright glimmer in his dark eyes. It made her nervous. She couldn't afford to let her guard down around him. Not now.

"Addie's Glen was the one good memory I took away from this place." Maryann swallowed the rest of what she wanted to say, determined to be mature about a past that was better forgotten.

She slipped off her heels and sat down in one of the Queen Anne chairs she'd shipped from New York. Of all the opulent furnishings in their elegant home, those two burnished golden chairs were the only things she'd brought with her.

Perhaps that was because she'd chosen them herself, without Terrence's overbearing decorator to tell her they weren't suitable for the glitz and glamour of her husband's chrome-and-glass penthouse masterpiece. Perhaps she kept them because these chairs represented freedom. Maryann wasn't sure herself. She only knew they'd been a comfort when, night after night, she'd sat by the window in her bedroom and looked out on Central Park, wondering if God could or would hear her if she prayed.

"The *only* good memory?" Clayton turned from the mural and frowned at her, drawing Maryann out of her reminiscences. "I have to wonder why you came back here, then. Surely it couldn't have been all bad?"

Maryann smiled her professional I-am-an-ice-maiden-you-can't-hurt-me smile. It slid into place automatically after years of practice. "No, of course it wasn't," she agreed quietly, averting her eyes from his probing look. "Silly me, I shouldn't have said that. Would you like some coffee? Tea?"

Now that was dumb. She wanted him gone, not sitting in her apartment, chatting about the good old days.

"No, thanks." He studied her for a few more moments, hands clenched at his sides. "Maryann, will you have dinner with me?"

Her head jerked up at the question. Go out with Clayton Matthews? Here? Now? Surprisingly enough, the idea appealed to her. And it shouldn't have.

"Why?" she blurted, and immediately lectured herself silently on the wisdom of controlling her tongue.

"To talk, to eat. I haven't seen you much since Caitlin and Jordan's wedding. You left right after Christmas. I was hoping we could spend some time together, but you were gone so fast."

She wouldn't tell him why, of course. There wasn't any point in explaining the paper she'd found, or the terror it had caused. But neither would she go out with him. Not tonight, especially not with all the reporters in town.

Not ever, she silently reminded herself.

"I'm sorry, Clayton, but I think I'd better stay in this evening and catch up on my rest." Which makes me sound like some kind of senior citizen! Maryann grimaced. "But thanks a lot for offering."

He nodded, his light brown hair glistening in the afternoon sun. "Where's Amy?"

Maryann wondered at his question. Her five-year-old daughter had no great love for Clayton, a fact Maryann didn't understand.

"Caitlin still has her downstairs. They wanted Amy to have some time with the baby, so they offered to keep her with them for the past couple of weeks while I stayed to finish up in the city."

Maryann kept her smile in place only through determination. Every bone in her body ached with the tension of returning from New York, every nerve twitched with the effort of maintaining this front of cool, calm control.

"Right. I forgot." He frowned. "You won't have anything in the place to feed her, then. I'll pick up some things, if you like. Have them delivered?" He smiled that grin she'd known since tenth grade. "I'm guessing you won't want to go back out with the piranhas there?"

She shuddered, thinking of the awful things they'd thrown at her, the hurtful insinuations. Problem was, most of those words held some element of truth.

"No, thanks, I don't want to go out." She hesitated, then berated herself for weakening. You wanted to avoid him, remember? she reminded herself. Maryann searched his kind face as the tiredness dragged at her body. "Are you sure you wouldn't mind picking up some milk and bread?" she finally managed.

"'Course not! No problem at all. You just give me a list and I'll get them. Hey, maybe we could eat here, together. Talk about old times?"

He looked so thrilled by the prospect, Maryann couldn't turn him down. Especially not when he was doing her a favor. There was no way she wanted to go outside again. Not tonight. She dredged her beneficent smile into place and nodded.

"That would be nice," she agreed calmly, then reminded herself that it wasn't Clayton's fault she'd isolated herself for so long.

She seldom ate with anyone but Amy anymore. Despite what the papers hinted, she'd purposely become a hermit in her private life. She liked it that way. If they couldn't get to you, they couldn't dig and probe and ask questions.

"I'll pick up a pizza. That way you won't have to cook. Where's your luggage?" Clay looked around, searching.

"Still in the car. I can get it later." Much later, she decided, suddenly remembering exactly what was in those leather cases.

"No way! I'll go get them now, and you can be unpacked before I get back. No point in dragging it out, is there?"

Maryann sighed. He looked so innocent, standing there in his chambray shirt and jeans, worn white spots on the knees and the elbows. Why hadn't she stayed here, all those years ago, and encouraged Clayton Matthews to fall in love with her? That would have been a real life.

"Maryann?"

"What? Oh. No," she mumbled, handing him the car keys. "No point in dragging it out at all."

He stared at her, obviously wondering what was wrong. She wouldn't tell him, of course. There wasn't any reason for him to know. There wasn't a reason for anyone to know. Especially not anyone here in Oakburn. She'd done enough by bringing her problems to this friendly, uncomplicated town.

By the time Clayton came back with her luggage, Maryann had changed out of her navy business suit and heels into a pair of soft comfortable corduroy jeans, a creamy acrylic sweater and tennis shoes. She felt infinitely better.

"Hey, that's a long sweater!" Clayton grinned when he pointed to her knees, almost hidden by the fisherman's knit. "Was it your husband's? You must miss him a lot."

"I must, mustn't I?" Maryann despised the caustic tone in her voice. She took the smaller case from him and allowed him to lug the larger one into her bedroom.

"No, this wasn't Terrence's," she finally replied civilly. "Mother sent it to me after Dad died two years ago. It was a Christmas gift I once gave him. He never got to wear it, but whenever I do, I think of him. Mom died six months ago, you know."

"I'm sorry. You've lost a lot of people in your life in a short time. It's good you have the memories though." Clayton took a cursory look around her bedroom and left, obviously uncomfortable with all the frills and lace she'd used to make it ultrafeminine.

Maryann followed his gaze. In the first few weeks of living at Wintergreen last fall, this room had been a balm to her soul. It was her place, hers alone. She was safe here. Nothing could touch her. Now, as she looked around, Maryann wondered if perhaps she'd overdone the rosebuds just a bit. She smiled as she trailed Clay out of the room, remembering the uncomfortable look on his face.

"I'll get going to the store." Clayton avoided her glance, and headed out the door, cap returned firmly to his head. "See you in a while."

"Clayton?"

He stopped and turned back, his eyes opened wide. "Yeah?"

"Thanks a lot for helping me out. I really appreciate it."

He blushed. That was the only word for it. A big, red, cheek-heating blush that made his eyes look even more deeply set. His hands fiddled with each other, dangling from his thickly corded arms. He looked like a nervous teddy bear, she decided. A wonderfully friendly bear who simply accepted a person for who she was. She needed that acceptance so badly.

"I mean it, Clay. Thank you."

"Not a problem, Mare." He saluted, grinned at the old nickname, then loped down the stairs like a pony anxious to get out to the paddock and run.

Maryann hurried through to Amy's bedroom and watched as the fifty or so reporters now outside Wintergreen's white picket fence flocked around him like flies on a steak.

"Not a problem for you," she muttered softly, talking to no one in particular. "You don't care about silly things like what people think. But a really big problem for me. I'll just have to hope it goes away."

It wouldn't, of course. At least not for the next few weeks. She had to face the fact that she was the story of the month. Disconsolate, Maryann returned to her bedroom.

By the time she'd unpacked and stored the papers at the back of her desk, the sun was sinking and the warm balmy spring air of the afternoon had turned chilly. Maryann lit a small fire and rubbed her hands as the flames flickered to life, thinking of all the things that had conspired to bring her to this point in her life's journey.

"Maryann? Are you home?" Caitlin's voice broke

through her maudlin reverie, and she gratefully shut it all out.

"Hi, Caitlin." Maryann moved across the room to open the door, then allowed the other woman to hug her. She returned it halfheartedly, feeling shy and out-of-place as she did so. How strange to be welcomed back so eagerly, as if she'd never left.

"Yes, I'm home. I rang earlier but no one answered. What's the matter? Isn't Amy with you?" Maryann peered around her friend, searching the hallway.

"That's the problem. She, uh, she won't come up here. When we came in, the reporters asked her if Clayton was going to be her new daddy, and she burst into tears. She says that if he's here, she's not coming up."

Deep down Maryann had known that the reporters would get to the child. She'd just hoped it would be later, when things were more settled. Why did God let this happen to her?

Of course, she knew the answer to that. She deserved it for her deceit. She swallowed and focused on the conversation at hand.

"You were such a peach to take her, Caitlin. And I know she's a handful. I'll come get her." Maryann moved to go through the door, but Caitlin's hand on her arm stopped her.

"What is Amy's problem with Clayton, Maryann? He's a nice guy. He really cares about both you and Amy."

"Amy's just ultrasensitive about men since her father's death. She'll get over it." Maryann held the door open, waiting for her friend to pass through.

Unfortunately Caitlin held her ground. "It can't be that simple. Are you sure there's nothing—?"

Caitlin broke off, her forehead wrinkled. "I'm prying, aren't I? Never mind, I'm sure Amy will be fine."

"Of course she will. My daughter is just as resilient as I am. It's just taking her a bit longer, that's all." Maryann forced a smile to her lips as she led the way down the stairs into Caitlin's home. "How's *your* daughter?"

"Micah's wonderful. I left her with Amy, sleeping."

"Good. That's what babies are supposed to do. Hello, darling!"

Maryann eagerly swept Amy's chubby little body into her arms and hugged tightly, whispering a prayer of thanks for this delightful child. Giving birth to Amy was the one right thing she'd done in her ill-chosen life plan. She wasn't going to mess that up now.

"Is he there?" Amy's big blue eyes searched her mother's face for a clue.

"Who, darling?" she asked, though Maryann knew exactly to whom her daughter referred.

"That man."

"Amy," her mother warned, setting the child down. "Clayton is very kind to help us out when we need him. He's our friend."

"He's not my friend. I don't like him." Amy stood firm, her face mutinous. "And you can't make me."

"No, I can't," Maryann agreed quietly. "But I wish you'd give him a chance. He really likes you. And once he was my very best friend, when I used to live here before." She smiled, brushing the child's cheek with her own. "Remember? I told you all about Caitlin and Beth and Clay. We all went to school together. We were friends."

"My friends are in New York. I want to go back there!"

Maryann stifled a sigh. Amy was singing her familiar tune, nagging about the wonders of her former home with its toy-stuffed playroom and the abundance of staff who waited on her hand and foot.

"Sweetheart, you've grown too big for that preschool. Those were just little kids. You're growing into a big girl. Soon you'll be starting kindergarten and you'll have new friends here in Oakburn."

"Don't want new friends."

From past experience, Maryann knew that five-year-old Amy wouldn't budge from this negative stance until she was ready. Now her face was set in a determined frown, lower lip jutting out just enough to warn Maryann that her daughter wouldn't listen to reason, at least not now.

"Amy, I need another diaper for Micah. Do you think you could run to her room and get me one? Oh, you're a doll!" Caitlin watched, a tiny smile playing about her lips, as the little girl nodded, then scampered inside the apartment to the second-floor nursery. "Did the reporters give you a rough time?"

Maryann shrugged, refusing to let her friend see how rattled all the prying made her. She followed Caitlin to the living room.

"I managed. Clayton helped me inside, past most of them." She sank into a chair and sighed. "I don't know how he knew to be there, but I'm sure glad he was." She knotted her fingers, her voice dropping.

"I suppose you've heard all the gossip?"

Caitlin nodded solemnly, her face sympathetic.

"Aren't you going to ask?" Maryann stiffened her spine, prepared for the worst.

"Ask what?" Caitlin laid her daughter Micah on the sofa, undid her sleeper, then her diaper and replaced it with the dry one Amy handed her. "Thank you, Amy." She waited until Amy wandered away before she looked up at Maryann.

"Anything you want to tell me will be held in strictest confidence, honey. But your marriage isn't any of my business."

"Not even if it was the biggest flop in history?" Maryann kept her voice soft, watching Amy climb onto the window seat and peer outside into the blooming garden. "Don't you long to say 'I told you so'?"

"Me?" Caitlin hooted. "I don't think so! I'm in no position to judge you. I've been too busy making my own goofs." She cooed at the baby and smiled at the string of bubbles that ensued. "I just want you to be happy. Are you?"

Caitlin fixed her with that no-nonsense look that wouldn't allow for prevarication. In ten years, Caitlin Andrews hadn't changed much. She still probed for the truth with a fierceness that made her friends wince. Maryann had to admit, she kind of liked that trait.

"I don't know." She shrugged. "I suppose I'm as happy as I can be."

"That doesn't sound very certain. What is it you're after, Maryann? You've got a wonderful daughter, there's a man around here who thinks you're the next best thing to pecan pie, and you paint like a dream. What more do you want?"

"Clayton Matthews doesn't have any feelings for me. He doesn't even know me. Not the real me." Maryann sighed. If he did, she thought, he'd run the other way.

"Of course he knows you." Caitlin made a face.

"You and Clay hung around together a lot in the old days. It made me so envious to see the two of you at Addie's." She shook her head. "I was jealous, I suppose. I wanted you to be friends with me and only me."

"I was, I *am* your friend, Caitlin!"

"I thought you were. But when you took off so fast after high school, I thought maybe I'd done something wrong. The next thing I knew you were married to some hotshot lawyer and living in the Big Apple. In those days I never dreamed you'd come back to little old Oakburn to live with *me*." Caitlin shook her head. "I guess that just goes to show how God directs our paths."

"Hmm. I guess. Though it never seemed to me like God's leading. Not really. Nothing's turned out as I expected." And wasn't that the understatement of the year! Maryann fiddled with her sweater.

"What *did* you expect when you moved into Wintergreen with Beth and me, Maryann?"

Caitlin looked really interested, so Maryann allowed just a tiny bit of her insecurity to shine through. "I thought I could come back here and be plain old Maryann MacGregor. I thought I could fit in, be one of the locals, raise my daughter and paint. I guess I never thought my past would follow me here the way it has."

Caitlin nodded, her glance thoughtful. "It's funny how that works," she murmured, playing with the baby's feet. "Just when you think it's dead and gone, the past has a habit of jumping up and biting you until you deal with it." She cocked an ear, nodded toward the hall and winked at Maryann.

"He's ba-a-a-ck," she singsonged, muffling a giggle.

Maryann listened to the off-key whistle Clay was known for and nodded. "Come on, Amy. Say thank you to Auntie Caity, and let's go get some dinner on the table."

Amy did her duty, pressed a kiss on the baby's temple and then skipped up the stairs, singing a little rhyme as she went. She stopped dead at the top when she saw Clayton, her red beret hanging lopsided over one ear.

"Hi, Amy. I brought your mom some groceries she needs. And a pizza." Clayton's big booming voice tumbled down the stairs.

"I hate pizza," Amy declared, and pushed past him to get inside the apartment.

"Well, I don't." Maryann motioned Clayton inside and closed the door behind her. "It smells wonderful!"

"We should eat it while it's hot," Clayton murmured, his glance moving from Maryann to her daughter. "Do you want me to go?" he asked.

"Yes!" Amy was vehement in her reply, proof positive that she hadn't been ignoring him as much as she wanted them to believe. "We both do."

"Amy Lou Arnold!" Maryann gasped at the little girl's rudeness. She tilted her head toward the bedroom. "I'd like to talk to you please, young lady."

The little girl stomped past her, and Maryann spared a rueful look for Clay.

"We'll be right back," she promised quietly.

Once inside Amy's bedroom, Maryann proceeded to read her daughter the riot act. "We do not treat our guests like that. Especially when they've been so kind to us. You will march out there and apologize properly, Miss Arnold.''

Amy glowered, her whole body leaning forward in a challenge. Her face was red, set in a rigid line of defiance.

''Now!'' Maryann refused to back down.

The child had been badly spoiled by Terrence while he was alive, and Maryann was determined to correct her rude behavior. She promised herself that she would not become a tyrant while doing so, but neither would she allow Amy to ride roughshod over other people's feelings. She met her daughter's angry look head-on, never wavering.

''I mean it, honey. You were terribly rude to my friend, and I won't accept that. He's been kind to us.''

''But we don't *need* him hanging around.''

''Sweetheart, we need all the friends we can get,'' Maryann countered softly. ''Apologize, please.''

After a few seconds Amy stomped her foot, then flounced out the door and down the hall to stand directly in front of Clayton, who was opening the pizza box.

''Sorry,'' the girl muttered, lips clenched together in a snarl.

''That's all right, Amy.'' Clayton smiled down at her.

To Maryann's amazement, he didn't seem put out by her daughter's pout, or her rebellion. He went on doing exactly what he'd started, his voice friendly but not gushing.

''I expect you have a lot to tell your mother. You've been staying downstairs with the Andrews, haven't you?'' He put the pizza in the center of the table, found the plates and silverware and set them out, then surveyed his handiwork, head tilted to one side.

"It must have been fun looking after the baby, though I get nervous when she cries. She always sounds so mad."

"That's because you don't know anything about babies." Scorn oozed from the five-year-old voice.

"Yeah," he agreed, nodding thoughtfully. "I guess you're right. My brothers were all older than me."

"I didn't know you got brothers." Amy frowned up at him, obviously trying to figure out this latest piece of information. "That's a family."

"Yes, it is." He smiled down at her and gently lifted the hat from her shoulder. "This was falling off."

Amy took the beret and tossed it onto the sofa, her forehead creased in thought.

Maryann took her place at the table as Clayton held her chair. She motioned to Amy, who stubbornly refused his assistance but then had to accept it anyway because she was too far from the table to reach the pizza.

The child sniffed when he lifted her closer, and muttered a 'thank you' that sounded less than heartfelt. But her fury did not extend to the pizza he'd brought. Two minutes later Amy was happily indulging herself.

"This is delicious," Maryann murmured, enjoying the feeling of warm food in her stomach after such a trying day. She'd completely forgotten about lunch, and breakfast was a hurried cup of coffee before six. "Thank you, Clayton."

"More breadsticks!" Amy cut across the conversation. She dared a look at her mother, swallowed and then murmured, "Please."

Clayton chuckled, passing the wicker basket with its fragrant bread. "You sure seem to like these. They're almost gone, and I don't think your mom has had one."

"She doesn't eat bread," Amy informed him. "She doesn't want to be fat like a cow."

Maryann bowed her head in mortification, the repeated words ringing around the room. What other awful things had Amy overheard and stored away in that inquisitive little mind of hers?

"That's a fallacy, you know." Clayton studied the little girl seriously.

Amy thrust her nose in the air, but her eyes were wide open with curiosity. "What's a fal—what you said?"

"It means people think something's true but it's not. Lots of people think cows are fat, but that isn't necessarily true. Cows have udders where they make and store milk, and that's what sometimes makes them look fat." He glanced up, noticed Maryann's eyes on him, and flushed. "Oh, sorry. I shouldn't be talking about farming at the table."

"I don't know why not." Maryann sipped the coffee she'd made earlier, thankful for his calm diffusion of the situation. "It's actually very interesting." She wanted the focus off them. "Do you have a lot of cows?"

"Not that many. My mother was the one who liked farm cream. I only kept them for her."

"I was sorry to hear about her death," Maryann murmured, thinking of the strong, forceful woman who'd been left with six boys and a mortgaged farm when her husband had abandoned his family one day after a crop failure caused by hail. "She was quite a woman."

"Yes, she was. She always said you were too. She said you were the type who had hidden layers of strength that no one would believe just by looking at you."

Maryann gulped. They'd discussed her?

"Uh, thank you." She munched on a piece of pineapple, searching for a neutral topic. "Where are your brothers now?"

"They all moved to the city. None of them wanted to farm. Bad memories, I guess. I think they were relieved when I took it over." He shrugged. "Like you and your sisters, they could hardly wait to get away from Oakburn. I don't remember Dad's leaving, so I suppose it didn't bug me so much to stay on the very farm that he couldn't hack."

"It must have been hard, though."

"Hardest for Mom, I think. And Steve and Kevin, they were the oldest. But there was too much to do to fuss for very long. We all had to pitch in. Eventually, we just learned to enjoy what we had. I've always loved it." He grinned.

Maryann smiled, enjoying the way his dark eyes snapped with excitement. She'd missed him, she realized. Missed the calm, simple pleasure he took from every facet of life. She glanced across the table and saw Amy studying him closely.

"The thrill of watching the seeds grow and mature always gets to me. The soil is such an affirmation of God's love."

"Dirt is an affirmation?" Maryann raised one eyebrow. "How?"

"It's always there, waiting to shelter, protect and

nurture life. You can dig it, freeze it, heat it—doesn't matter. It's still waiting for the seeds.''

"Thank you for the good pizza.'' Amy piped up beside them.

Maryann started. For a moment she'd forgotten the child, hadn't even been aware of the fact that her daughter had left her chair and was now standing beside Clayton's, regarding him sternly.

"You're welcome.'' He grinned. "I'm sorry you had to eat something you hate.'' He winked at Maryann.

"It was okay. You'd better go now.'' The little girl's voice was firm with reproof. "My dad doesn't like it when there are strangers in our family. My mom's not s'posed to ask people for supper. If you're here, he'll be really mad.''

"But, but...'' Clayton's face grew red as he blustered over the words.

"Goodbye,'' Amy murmured, holding out his hat. When Clay didn't move she tugged on his arm, her face scrunched up with worry. "You have to go *now*.''

Maryann gaped, her stunned eyes noting the furrowed eyebrows and whitened cheeks on her daughter's round face. The little girl was serious.

Oh, no! Maryann groaned as reality penetrated her brain.

Amy still believed her daddy was alive.

Chapter Two

"Sweetheart, you know that daddy died, don't you? He's gone. Don't you remember?" Maryann stared at her daughter's mutinous face, willing her to accept what had happened many months ago.

"I remember, Mommy. But he didn't go. He said he wouldn't ever leave me." Amy's bottom lip jutted out in defiance. "He promised!"

Maryann swallowed her dismay. This was no time to indulge in self-pity. Obviously Amy hadn't grasped the finality of her father's death, even though she'd witnessed Terrence Arnold's collapse, visited him in the hospital and attended the funeral.

"I think I'd better go." Clayton's voice was calm, but concern glowed in his eyes. "Will you be all right?" His hand on her arm, he assisted Maryann to her feet.

"Yes, of course."

Maryann kept her voice down, even though Amy, after one baleful glare at that proprietary touch, moved off into the living room to stare out the window. Maryann was grateful Clay didn't ask any questions.

"I guess I'll have to talk to her about Terrence's death again." She frowned. "It's just that I was so sure she understood that her father wouldn't be coming back. I thought she'd accepted it when he didn't come out of the coma."

"I'm sure you'll handle it perfectly." He reached out and squeezed her shoulder. "May I take you to the church garage sale on Saturday?"

Maryann shook her head. She hated to do it. Clayton was kind, thoughtful and understanding. He had listened to her all those years ago at Addie's, just as he'd listened tonight.

But she couldn't confide in him now. Not about her marriage, not about the future. Not even about Amy. She couldn't afford to let him get close. She'd only have to push him away again.

"I'm sorry, Clayton. But I don't think it's a good idea. Obviously Amy is going to need some help accepting her father's death. And since she doesn't, um..." She searched for some way to put it politely.

"Since she seems to hate me," he supplied helpfully, his mouth tilted to one side in a grin. "Is that what you're trying to say?"

"Well, not hate, I'm sure. But she does have strong feelings, and I need to deal with them, find out what's at the bottom of it all. I just don't think it's a good idea to go anywhere with you or anyone else right now. And then, there are the reporters."

"Yeah, the reporters. Okay, another time." He turned away, but Maryann stopped him, one hand on his muscular forearm.

"No, Clayton. I'd like us to remain friends, but—well, I think that's all it can ever be."

He glanced at her hand on his arm. Then his eyes moved to study her face, searching for an answer that she wouldn't, couldn't give him.

"Friends, real friends, tell one another when there's a problem." His voice was serious. "What's bothering you, Maryann? Ever since you first came here last winter, you've been different. You rushed away without saying a word after Christmas. Now you're back, but you don't look as if anything's been resolved. You seem worried or something. Can't I help?"

Tears ached behind her eyelids. He was such a nice man. And she had been such a fool! He would never understand why she'd made the decisions she had, why she intended to live a lie.

"No, thanks, Clayton. I've got to deal with this in my own way. But I appreciate your concern. You're a good friend. Anyway, you don't want to bother with me. I hear you have other fish to fry." She stood on tiptoe and brushed her lips against his cheek.

His eyes opened wide at the caress. "I do?"

"So I hear." She smiled, relieved that the focus was once more off her. "Melanie Pickering, wasn't it? Or Melinda Samuels?" She grinned. "You have a busy life."

"I'm not dating them," he told her candidly, two red spots glowing high on his cheekbones. "They're just friends."

"Then so am I. Three M-friends! That's a new record, even for you." She saw the glow deep in his eyes, and looked away.

"It's different with you, Mare. It always has been."

The smile slipped from her lips. She couldn't deal

with this. Not now. If he ever found out what she was going to do, Clayton Matthews would never even look at her again. He was honest and principled in everything he did. He would never understand the deliberately deceitful action she planned to carry out.

Besides, Clay had her on a pedestal. Maybe it was selfish, but she didn't want to spoil his illusions with reality. Not yet. "We can only be friends, Clayton. That's all."

"And after you've grieved? Once you're past his death?"

She had to squash that hopeful look on his face. There just wasn't any other way. "I think I am over Terrence's death. After he had that stroke, he was in a coma for three months, and I had time to accept the inevitable. I was prepared when he passed away. But that doesn't change anything. I won't ever marry again. I don't want that in my life."

"You won't even give me a chance? You won't see if we could rebuild what we once had? Why? What is it that you're so afraid of that you've run halfway across the country to avoid?"

"I'm not running away. I'm just trying to build a new life for my daughter and me." She avoided his knowing look.

"Yeah, right! You wouldn't talk to me ten years ago either, and I was crazy in love with you then. Instead you ran away. Why, Maryann? Why do you always run from me?"

She couldn't deal with this romanticized picture he still held of her as some tragic figure, couldn't answer one more question. Couldn't endure the awful regret that swept over her every time she remembered what she'd given up and what she'd gained in return.

Why couldn't he let things be? Why did he have to keep probing? She felt like a rabbit backed into a corner. Desperately her mind searched for a way out.

"Do you want to know why I left? The real reason?"

It would hurt him, and she didn't want to do that—but there was no other choice. Clayton knew too much about her already. He couldn't be allowed to learn any more.

He nodded slowly. "The truth."

"Fine. Here's the truth, Clayton. I wanted out of this town. I hated being poor, I hated being one of the eight MacGregor kids whose parents could barely keep the wolf from the door. I hated everything about my life, and I sure wasn't going to drudge away on a farm, scraping and scrimping for every dime. I wanted more than that."

Inside she winced at the tortured look on his face, but she kept going, determined that he see how truly ugly she was inside.

"It didn't matter that you thought you loved me, Clayton. It didn't weigh into the balance. I wanted nice clothes, a house that I wasn't ashamed of, decent shoes that weren't someone's cast-offs. I figured life owed me, and I decided to make it pay."

She turned away, checking on Amy as she did. Fortunately, the child had grown tired of her vigil at the window. Now she lay, curled in a little ball, fast asleep on the sofa, beret clutched in one hand.

"Love didn't have anything to do with my decisions. I married Terrence Arnold because he could give me all those things. Money, prestige, power—Terrence had all of that. That's the whole truth about my marriage.'' She shrugged, pretending a carelessness she didn't feel.

''You make it sound like a business arrangement.''

She smiled sadly. ''Perhaps it was. Now I have a daughter, and I intend to devote myself to loving her and raising her so that she feels secure, so that she won't make the same mistakes I did. I can't focus on more than that right now, Clayton. Okay?''

He stood transfixed, his posture rigid, his eyes dark and whirling with something she couldn't even guess at. His hands, balled into fists at his sides, opened and closed uselessly. She could see the muscle in his jaw flicker.

He was hurt and angry.

''If that's what you wanted, if *things* were so important to you,'' he grated from between clenched teeth, ''then what are you doing back here in Oakburn? Why come back to everything you despised?''

Maryann didn't look away, didn't flinch, didn't give him a glimpse into the maelstrom that boiled up inside. She didn't dare. ''I came back to raise my daughter in a safe, familiar place,'' she whispered. ''That's all.''

He let out a deep, pent-up breath of air. As she watched, Maryann marveled at the way he discarded his tension like a snake shedding its skin. The lines of strain around his mouth eased, his fingers flexed, his feet shuffled. When she met his gaze, she got caught in the eddies of those glossy velvet eyes and remembered how they'd once glowed for her.

''I don't think so,'' he said, clearly and concisely.

Maryann jerked back to the present, her mind spinning. ''Pardon?''

''I don't think that's the only reason you're back. You could have raised Amy anywhere. You're looking

for something, Maryann. Something you didn't find in
New York.'' He nodded, more to himself than to her
as he talked the idea through.

''No. I—''

He simply smiled and kept speaking. ''You came
running back home because you thought you'd left
that something here, and you wanted to get it back.
You always did think running was the answer.''

She shook her head, her mouth opening. But he cut
her off again.

''I'm right, Mare. And you know it.'' He grinned,
that smug, self-assured smile that was a Matthews
hallmark. ''Coming home was the right thing to do,
Maryann. This is where you belong. Now all I have
to do is convince you of that.''

''Didn't you hear anything I said?'' she sputtered,
annoyed by the flash of amusement across his face.

''Yeah, I heard.'' He grinned.

''And?''

''And I'm still here. You didn't scare me off any
more than Amy did. You'll just have to accept it,
Mare. I'm not going anywhere. Whether you like it or
not, you'll have to face me day in and day out. I'm
going to be here so often, you'll even stop noticing
that I'm around.''

The very idea was ridiculous. She could no more
ignore Clayton than she could stop breathing. But that
was only because he reminded her of what could have
been.

Wasn't it?

Clayton moved closer, his face within inches of
hers. His voice was low and commanding.

''Ten years ago, I goofed. I should have told you
straight up front that I wanted to marry you. I should

have reminded you last winter when you first moved back, but I let you keep me at arm's length. Instead, I hinted and hoped.'' He shrugged.

Maryann gulped. He'd wanted to marry her? ''I was newly widowed. I needed time.''

''And I gave it to you. Maybe too much time.'' He shrugged. ''Okay, that's in the past. But I'm telling you now, Maryann MacGregor. I care for you. And whether you like it or not, whatever secrets you're keeping, my feelings aren't going to change.''

He kissed her quickly, as if anticipating her objections. When Maryann finally blinked her eyes open, Clayton was standing at the door.

''The past we might have shared is gone, Mare. We can't do anything about that. But we've got today. And we've got the future. We can make a brand-new start. That's exactly what I aim to do.'' He grinned, saluted and then he was gone, his boots clomping heavily down the stairs.

Maryann touched her lips wonderingly. He'd sounded so sure!

But then, of course, Clayton didn't know what she was about to do. He had no idea that anyone could be less than upright and straightforward in their dealings because he was so totally scrupulous. He didn't know she was a cheat.

Maryann moved across the apartment as if in a trance, sliding the supper dishes into the sink, disposing of the cardboard pizza box. With the kitchen tidy, she moved to rouse her daughter. She tucked Amy into bed, dutifully prayed with her, wishing the words had more meaning for them. Then she waited until Amy's little eyes drooped shut before returning to her desk, staring at it as if it was alive, knowing the telltale pieces of paper lay inside, hidden, eating away at her heart.

Slowly she pulled out the folder, opened it and unfolded the single sheet of heavy white bond paper enclosed within. Why had Terrence left this for her to find after his death? Why had he complicated her life so badly?

Why did I ever find this awful letter in his office? How am I supposed to deal with this, God?

As she studied the scrawling words, Maryann's heart contracted into a cold, hard, lump.

Maryann,

If you've found this, you know the truth. I never wanted it to be this way. I never intended to hurt or embarrass you or Amy. I love my daughter, you know that.

It sounds ridiculous to say I've finally found true love at this stage of my life, but that's the truth. As God is my witness, Celine isn't just a fling, a dalliance of a foolish older man. She really cares for me. And I love her more than I thought I would ever love anyone. I never expected to find such joy.

If we're honest, Maryann, you and I never shared love. I cared for you, tried to make you happy, but there was no real love. You wanted safety, security and the things you'd missed out on for so long. I liked being able to give those to you. But after a while, it wasn't enough. When I met Celine again, I realized why.

Nothing I can say here will assuage my guilt or make things easier for you, but I cannot renege on my duty to Celine. I do not wish either her or her child to be destitute. After all, it will be my baby too.

If I die, please divide whatever is left of my estate equally between yourself and Celine. I've chosen not to include this in my will because I don't want to cause you any public distress. Neither will I force you to act through codicils or other legal means. You must do as you think best for everyone concerned.

The decision is yours, Maryann. Make it because you've realized you don't need me or my money any longer. In truth, you never did. You could have managed just fine. By now I'm sure you've learned what it took me so long to understand. True happiness doesn't come from money or the things it buys. And love cannot be arranged like a business merger. I pray one day you will find real true love and share it with a man who deserves you far more than I ever did.

Until then, take good care of my daughter. Remind her always that her daddy loved her.

Terrence.

Slowly, carefully, Maryann folded the paper and returned it to its envelope. Then she closed the folder and slid it into the drawer, to the very back.

How could he have betrayed her like that? He must have known there wouldn't be much left when he made those monthly withdrawals. How could he take from them and give to Celine? Maryann felt the tears, hot and painful, burn in her throat. Terrence's betrayal went far beyond the mere physical. He'd betrayed her spiritually.

It was up to her. He'd said it was her decision. No

one knew about his paper. There was nothing anyone could do so long as she kept it hidden, ignored the words.

"You were wrong, Terrence," she said out loud. "You were so wrong. How will we live without an income to keep a roof over our heads, to give Amy the things she needs and wants? How will I make sure Amy has everything a little girl should have to grow up happy and carefree?"

Maryann pushed away from the desk and moved to the window to stare out into the darkness of the night faintly lit by the patio lights that glimmered below.

She considered the words once more, knowing exactly what they meant. If she followed his directions, if she obeyed his request, every dream she'd ever held precious would be dashed to the ground like crystal shattered into a thousand glittering shards. She would have nothing—a bare subsistence. She'd be like her parents, scraping for the next dollar to pay the bills. Fear coiled inside her, ready to spring.

Why? Why had he done this to them? And what did he mean, she didn't need his money? Wasn't that the reason she'd married him in the first place, because he was a good provider? She hadn't lied about that. Now he'd left her with a child and a request that would deny Amy what her father owed her: the right to security.

Maryann eyed the fireplace longingly, but shook her head. Not yet. Not until every other solution had been exhausted. She knew she would burn the papers eventually, of course. She had to. They were the only barrier between her and the future she'd planned—a future free of worry.

But something told her that the agony of those

words would linger inside her heart long after the ashes had blown away.

"Brothers and sisters, let's give a warm hand of welcome to our returned sister, Maryann MacGregor, back with us at Oakburn First Avenue. And this time we hope it's for good!"

Maryann blinked in startled awareness as the entire church rose and began clapping. Hands reached out from all around, grasping hers, patting her shoulder, greeting the lost sheep back into the fold.

Reverend Willoughby hugged her as if she were his missionary daughter Evangeline, returned home after a twenty-year absence. Maryann, on the other hand, had been back in Oakburn for several weeks now. It was just that this was the first time she'd made it to church.

"Thank you very much. Yes, it's nice to be home. Thank you, I will."

She smiled at the offers of lunch and coffee. Just before she turned back to the front, her attention snagged for an instant on Clayton. He sat three rows behind, his eyes concentrated intently on her. It was a lovely spring morning with a refreshing breeze moving through the church, but suddenly Maryann felt hot. Though she pivoted to the front and kept her attention on the minister, she could feel Clay's stare penetrating through her navy sundress, deep to her very heart and soul.

She'd been out only a few times over the past few weeks, sneaking out through the back door in disguises she changed from one time to the next. Eventually, cheated of their quote and alerted to another bigger, better story, another victim to hound, the reporters slowly dispersed.

Clay's cool regard made their scrutiny seem rank and amateurish.

"Mommy, that man is watching us again." Amy's loud voice carried over the music that swelled and sank in the melody of an old familiar hymn.

Maryann flushed as several heads turned in their direction, smiling at the little girl decked out in her Sunday best. Amy's predilection for hats had been indulged by her father to the extent that she now had one for every occasion. Today she'd chosen a big straw hat with a fat yellow bow that draped down the back of her matching dress.

"Mommy? Did you hear me?" Amy's strident tones grew louder, just as both the organ and piano ceased.

"Yes, darling. Quiet now. The pastor is speaking." Maryann shifted in her seat, unable to find a comfortable spot. Why was Clay embarrassing her like this?

Amy finally settled into the pew, her eyes peering at the gray-haired preacher. She seemed to listen to the Scripture reading for a few moments, but then climbed onto her haunches, her mouth just inches from Maryann's ear.

"I don't like him."

Maryann winced. There's no way Clay could have missed that shrill, decisive condemnation, she decided. Not that it seemed to have much effect. When she glanced back, Clayton was still staring at her, a tiny smile curving the corners of his lips.

She hushed Amy up and pretended she was listening to the sermon, which, ironically, was on forgiveness.

"'And when you stand praying, if you hold anything against anyone, forgive him, so that your Father in heaven may forgive you your sins.'''

That was rich, Maryann mused. She couldn't forgive *herself*, so it was a cinch that God wouldn't. She also couldn't forgive Terrence.

She shoved the hurtful thought away and studied the bouquet of flowers that lent the old wood in the church a fresh new spring look. Casting a baleful glance around, Maryann decided that this building hadn't changed much. Most of the people who'd been here when her family lived here were still attending this church. Some had even asked about her siblings before the service started.

She wondered how much they remembered. Had they been curious about how such a big family had managed to make ends meet on the salary of a caretaker? She'd pretended, naturally. *Life was grand. They'd had love.* The old lines irritated her.

"Beloved, we must remember that 'humility and fear of the Lord bring wealth and honor and life.' That is, if we keep our priorities straight, God will make sure that the rest is taken care of."

Anger burned inside at the pat answer. Maryann wanted to stand up and shout, "That isn't always true! My parents were the most humble people around, and no one feared the Lord more than my dad. But he was the poorest of the poor."

She swallowed the words, fingers knotting in annoyance.

"Of course, the Bible isn't referring to just mere physical wealth, it's talking about our spiritual wealth in Jesus. It's something that neither moths nor rust can corrupt, the Word tells us. Beloved, let's get our eyes off the physical and onto the spiritual. Let's focus on the most important thing of all, the love of Christ.''

Maryann felt the sting of those words to the bottom of her feet. The most important thing—love. She stood with the entire congregation, but her mind was busy with the past. Had there really been another choice for her? Was there one now?

"Remember, dear ones, 'The house of the righteous contains great treasure, but the income of the wicked brings them trouble.'"

When benediction was finished and the congregation dwindling, Maryann became aware of her daughter tugging at her arm. "What is it, darling?"

"It's him! He's coming over here! Mommy, remember what Daddy said?"

Maryann sighed. She'd patiently tried to help Amy understand that Terrence was gone, he wasn't coming back. But the little girl was clinging to her belief like barnacles to a boat. She would not be moved from her insistence that Terrence was hanging around, just waiting to reappear in their lives. Obviously, her idea of the after-life needed clarification.

"What did Daddy say, honey?" Maryann couldn't understand this continued reference to something Terrence had told their child. Perhaps it was best to get it out in the open now, before things got carried away even further.

"You know!" Amy was whispering, her blue eyes huge as saucers.

"Sweetie, I don't know what you're talking about." Maryann loosed the fingers clenched around her arm and held them in hers. "What did Daddy tell you?"

Amy glanced around, spied Clayton less than two steps away, and clamped her jaw tight. Her voice was barely audible when she finally spoke. "He said he'd never leave us. That means he's here, waiting for us to be a fam'ly. I don't want Daddy to see you with *him,*" she muttered, spots of red dotting her cheeks.

"Sweetheart, Daddy's in heaven. He's busy with God and the angels. The things that happen here don't bother him because he knows we'll be okay. Do you understand?"

"Uh-huh." Amy hung her head, peering at her shoes.

"Hello, Maryann. Hi, Amy. You both look lovely today." Clayton's smile was warm and kind and it was hard to look away. That open-handed friendship wasn't something you brushed off easily.

"Hello." Maryann gathered up her purse and took Amy's hand. She stepped forward, intent on escaping the confines of the sanctuary before he said anything more. She knew what was coming.

He didn't disappoint her. "I was hoping you two would join me for lunch somewhere. There's a new place out by Emma Lake. They have a great menu." He looked so hopeful that it seemed a shame to deflate his balloon.

But Maryann couldn't take any chances. She had to stay away from Clayton Matthews, or risk getting drawn back into the same whirlwind she'd run away from ten years ago. This time, however, there wasn't any place to run.

"That's really kind of you, Clayton. And we appreciate the offer. But Amy and I had something planned for this afternoon. I'm sorry."

Funny, but she actually was sorry they wouldn't be going with him. Clayton could make her laugh, and a good laugh was exactly what she needed right now. That and a diversion from Amy's sullen silence.

"That's okay. Maybe I could tag along." He grinned at her surprised look. "You know, help finish lunch, clean up the crumbs, stuff like that."

"My mom and I have to go now." Amy's blue eyes burned with anger as she tried to move past. "'Scuse me."

"Sure, Amy. Not a problem." He took Maryann's arm as she moved down the steps, then stood there for a moment, waiting. There was a speculative look in his eyes that rattled her, and she averted her gaze. "I'll probably see you later this afternoon."

"Clayton, today really isn't a good time for us."

"Oh, I don't mean for a date or anything. It's just that I need to finish a few odd jobs at Wintergreen, and your cupboards happen to be one of them."

"Finish a few odd—you mean you're the one who renovated the staircase and redid those hardwood floors?" She remembered the silky smooth patina that glistened against the soft white area rugs she'd laid down only last week. Her forehead creased at this new information.

"Yep, that's me. It's a hobby I took up a while ago. Restoration is fun, and I can do a lot of it in the winter when I have more spare time."

"But it's finished now, right?" If there was a shade too much hope in the question, Clayton pretended not to notice.

"Almost. I've still got a few odd jobs here and there. The trim on the countertops is ready to be applied, and I have the new doors for the cabinets ready to hang."

"Oh." There wasn't much Maryann could say. The

house was Caitlin's, and she was just a renter. Still, she'd assumed most of the work had already been done. No one had mentioned new cabinet doors.

"So, see you later this afternoon, then. 'Bye, Amy."

He sauntered across the lawn with an assuredness that sent a little thrill down her spine. Clayton wasn't blessed with a lot of social graces. He and his brothers had grown up wrestling each other, and punching miscreants in the chops to enforce their points. Mrs. Matthews had tried, but six boys was a tough job for any woman.

But as she watched him stride across the church lawn, Maryann thought she'd never seen anyone move with such a relaxed, easy confidence. It was the sign of an innocent mind, she decided. Clayton Matthews had no reason to hide and run away, to seclude himself in a few rooms where no one could find him, or ask questions. He didn't fight against fate or blame God for his problems. He just got on with the job of living as best he could.

She, on the other hand, had several compelling reasons to avoid people. And the most important one was standing right here, by her side.

I won't risk my daughter or her future by getting too close to anyone again, she thought as Amy ran off to talk to several other children. Terrence's words resurfaced in her mind, reminding her that she stood to lose everything.

Apparently, with Clayton gone, Amy's worries disappeared. Which reminded Maryann that she was going to have to talk to her daughter. Again.

She hoped this time Amy would explain why she was so positive her father was waiting to come back, and why she was so afraid Clayton would ruin it all.

Chapter Three

"Faith in God can move a mighty mountain."

Clayton whimsically debated whether or not he could categorize Maryann as a *mighty* mountain as he hummed the tune on his way into town. She wasn't very big for a mountain. But, as he knew from the old days, her will was like granite.

He pulled up to the curb in front of Wintergreen and climbed down from his truck. One last check ensured that his boots were clean. He still had on his best jeans, even though he was supposed to be here to work, and his shirt wasn't wrinkled too badly after changing that flat. It would have to do.

He pressed the buzzer and waited, shifting nervously from one foot to the other.

"You again! What is it with you, man?" Jordan pretended a fierceness that fooled no one in Oakburn. "You thinking of moving in here or something?"

"I might." Clayton sniffed as he walked through the foyer and into the Andrews' home. "Is that roast beef I smell?"

"Yes," Jordan hissed. "And you're not having any. I have big plans with my wife for tonight, and you are not going to spoil them, Clayton. Now what do you want?"

It wasn't all pretend, Clayton decided. He sensed a hint of frustration in the other man's voice, and recalculated. Jordan angry wasn't a pretty sight.

"To see Caitlin. She told me to come over around three." He checked his watch. "It's twenty after. Is that a problem?"

"You need a woman of your own, Matthews. Caitlin is already taken. By me."

"He knows that, you nut!" Caitlin swatted at Jordan's shoulder with her tea towel, her eyes full of laughter. "Boy, I never had anyone fight over me before. This is really flattering." A low guttural noise emanating from Jordan's tanned and muscular throat showed he didn't share her delight. "Honey, I asked Clayton to build me a shelving unit. He did such a nice job with the kitchen that I decided to add an entertainment unit here." She motioned to the east wall.

Clayton whipped out his tape measure. "How big?" he asked, sizing up the area.

"I can build it." Jordan stood, glaring at them. "I can put together those prepackaged things as well as he does."

Clayton stifled his laughter and pointed to the wall behind the sofa. "With all due respect, my man, your last effort at hanging a picture cost forty-three dollars and ten cents to repair." He satisfied himself that no one could spot where the gaping hole had occurred before turning back to the glowering husband.

Jordan frowned even harder, his mouth opening and closing.

"And also, for your information, this isn't going to be any prefab unit. I'm going to build it from scratch."

"That hole was an accident!" Jordan's affronted look made Caitlin giggle. "There should have been a stud there."

"We know, darling. But still, building things is what Clayton does. And I really want an entertainment unit that I can close the doors on. Micah will soon be poking and probing into everything. Didn't you hear the MacAlisters talking about the cheese sandwich their son shoved into the VCR?"

She stopped and listened as the baby monitor on the coffee table squealed. "Ah, Miss Muffet has awakened. As usual, her timing is off."

"Micah is perfect," Jordan insisted, nose in the air as he crossed the room. His cheeks blazed bright red. "Just like me. I'll get her."

"He's not really mad, is he?" Clayton didn't like the thought of coming between a man and his wife, not even in pretend. Especially not Caitlin and the man who'd finally banished the shadows from her eyes. And Jordan was his friend; he had no desire to hurt him.

"Don't fall for it, Clay. He's using us," Caitlin laughed. "He'll pretend his feelings are hurt, and then he'll try to con me into doing something that he's already decided on. You have to know Jordan like I do to understand his mind."

"I heard that." Jordan returned with Micah snuggied against his chest, his face soft with love as he peered down at the little girl. "We know when we're not wanted, don't we, sweetheart? Let's go for a walk." In a matter of seconds he had the baby bundled in a blanket and ensconced in the stroller, which he adeptly wheeled out the door.

"Get your own wife, Matthews," he ordered before yanking the door closed behind him. The resounding *bang* carried the faintest hint of a threat.

"Now he's pretending he's mad." Caitlin chuckled. "Don't look so worried."

"It's not as if I'm not trying to get a wife," Clayton muttered, his face burning. "She doesn't want anything to do with me."

"Really? I noticed the two of you talking this morning. I didn't get that impression at all." Caitlin took the end of the measure and held it against the wall at the far end. She waited until Clayton had scribbled down the measurement and then offered a chair for him to stand on to take the height.

"She was telling me to get lost. Oh, not in those terms. Maryann's too fancy these days to say something like that. But I got the message." He smiled, remembering her face as he climbed back down from the chair. "She almost gasped when I told her I was the one who'd worked on her apartment. You can be sure I've got lots left to do too."

Caitlin shook her head, her face rueful. "I can see Jordan's not the only one who's into con games. I thought you'd finished up there while she was away?"

"Nope. Unfortunately, some of the supplies didn't come in when I expected. Then there was a lot to do on the farm, and one thing after another came up. I just got 'round to it. Since she wasn't there, I figured it could wait."

"And now, with seeding under way, I suppose you'll just have to fit it in whenever you can. An afternoon here, an evening there?'' Caitlin's eyes glimmered with mirth.

Clayton nodded, a well of pure happiness springing up inside. "I guess so. After all, I can't just abandon the farm, now can I?''

"Certainly not!'' Caitlin stood, hands on her hips, tongue in cheek. "That wouldn't do at all.''

"That's why I'm not too sure just when I'll be able to get this cabinet done,'' he offered, grateful for the understanding gleam in her eye.

"Oh, I empathize completely! After all, we wouldn't want Maryann to have to make do with an unfinished apartment, now would we?''

"I figured you'd grasp my situation.'' He pulled a sketch he'd made out of his pocket and laid it on the coffee table.

"Oh, I understand only too well, Clay. I just hope Maryann doesn't. I don't think she wants much company right now. She seems a little…I don't know. Nervous?''

Caitlin frowned, motioning toward the window. They watched Maryann and Amy stroll up the front walk. The little girl was chattering a mile a minute, her legs churning the air as she raced to keep up to her mother's stride.

"Look at that. She seems to be paying attention to Amy, but her mind is far away.'' Caitlin frowned.

"She's worried about something.'' Clay wished he hadn't said it, but in a way he was glad he had. He needed to talk to someone, and Caitlin was the best listener he knew.

Besides, he didn't have a clue how girls' minds worked. He'd tried to figure them out over the years, but just when he thought he was making progress, they'd burst out bawling or stomp off in a huff. Eventually, he'd learned to back off and keep his mouth shut whenever any female asked him for an opinion.

That didn't happen much anymore. Clayton figured he'd sort of bottomed out in the dating department. Almost all the women in town figured he was too staid to bother trying to change, and he wasn't about to try to alter that opinion. He had friends, he went out when it suited him. But most of the girls he'd known in school were now married and settled down with husbands and families of their own.

Having a steady date didn't bother him overly much then, and it didn't now. Not really. The only girl he'd ever wanted was Maryann MacGregor, and she'd only ever wanted him as a tutor and a friend. Lately, she didn't seem to want him around at all.

"Maryann? Worried? What do you mean?" Caitlin sat hunched over in her chair, studying the sketch Clayton had passed her. She squinted her eyes half-closed and held the paper up against the wall, trying to visualize what the room would look like finished.

"I don't know exactly. It's just that whenever she talks about the past or her husband, she gets this look on her face. As if she's scared I'll find out something she doesn't want me to know. It's a kind of guilty look."

"Maryann MacGregor? Miss Goody Two-Shoes?" Caitlin made a face that took the sting out of her words—she was only teasing. "What would somebody like her have to feel guilty about? She's had everything every woman could want. Money, trips, jewels, celebrity status, designer clothes, and yet she's as friendly as if she'd never left."

"I know."

"She doesn't even look like the old Maryann, Clay. She's so refined and polished. Remember in the old days, how her eyes used to kind of frost over when she was mad?"

"Yeah, she did that at your wedding. She can freeze you out with one look." Clay shook his head ruefully. "She doesn't do that anymore, though. She just gives you that polite, meaningless smile and goes on with what she was doing. Nothing seems to get to her lately."

Caitlin studied him with a frown. "And I take it you want to? 'Get to her,' I mean? You haven't changed your mind?"

Clayton grinned, sketching in the rest of the room for future reference. "No way! I figure I've been in love with that woman for about half my life. I'm not changing things now."

Caitlin was silent so long that Clay finally looked up from his drawing. Her face peered up at him seriously, her eyes soft.

"She might not come around," she warned. "If even half of what the papers say is true, she's gone through some pretty tough times."

"The papers! All they do is spread lies. I checked into Terrence the Great. He got a pretty good rating, according to most of his friends. He was well liked, a good business man, provided for his family, loved his daughter. He had everything. A guy like that wants quality around him, not some sleazy affair. And Maryann is quality."

"There might be more to their story than that. Something she doesn't want anyone to know about. You have to be careful, Clay. She won't like it if she finds out you've been poking into her life."

Caitlin wasn't looking at him. Instead, her eyes were focused out the window, watching a man who stood across the street snapping photos of Maryann and Amy picking a handful of wild daisies that grew by the fence.

Clay followed her gaze. He sputtered, then got to his feet when the reporter edged a little closer. "Why don't they leave her alone?" he seethed. "I'll teach them—"

Caitlin grabbed his arm and held on. "Sit down," she ordered, and didn't let go until he did. "You'll only add to the gossip by running out there and creating a scene. A picture of her and her daughter picking flowers isn't going to generate nearly as much speculation as you punching out some reporter."

She was right. Clayton forced his temper to cool, his hands to unclench. Maryann wasn't in any danger. And she sure wouldn't appreciate his jumping in and causing a scene.

They waited and watched, and after a few minutes mother and daughter came inside. He could hear Amy thundering up the stairs, her voice bellowing out a chorus from church.

"Are you still here?" Jordan thundered from the doorway. At the sound of his loud voice, Micah jerked and gave a cry. Daddy Jordan went from grump to comforter in microseconds, tenderly calming the little girl in his big embrace.

"That's all right, Sweet Pea. Clayton won't do that anymore. He just doesn't understand about little girls."

"I sure don't. Amy acts as if I'm the grim reaper whenever I come around. I wish I knew what was bothering her. She keeps saying her father's coming back.''

He saw Caitlin and Jordan share a look.

"What?'' Clay demanded. "Why are you looking like that?''

"There was an article in the paper this morning that might shed some light on that,'' Jordan muttered, handing Micah to her mother. "Where is that paper, Lyn?''

"There, under the sofa cushion where you stuffed it when I told you it was time to go to church.'' She stuck her tongue in the side of her cheek at his surprised look. "Did you think—no, *hope* I wouldn't notice, Jordan?'' she asked sweetly.

"Busted!'' He threw his hands up in the air, his eyes wide open as they met Clayton's. "Okay, what do I owe?''

A smile of pure delight curved across Caitlin's face. "Two weeks of cleaning the bathroom.'' Her eyes sparkled with glee.

"Aw, come on, Caitlin!'' Jordan took the baby from her and handed Micah to Clayton. "You don't want to inflict cruel and inhuman punishment like that. You love me, remember?'' His hands closed around her shoulders, but Caitlin wasn't budging.

"I *don't* love cleaning newsprint off the cushions, Jordan. And I have asked you before,'' she reminded. "Numerous times.''

Clayton jiggled the baby, hoping she wouldn't start squealing before his two friends got this latest difficulty ironed out. He didn't actually understand any of it, but he knew that Jordan would try to wheedle his way out. Jordan was not fond of cleaning of any sort.

"I know—but, sweetheart! Two weeks! That's torture.'' True to form, Jordan tried to cuddle and, cajole her. He even tried to kiss her.

Clayton turned his back, carrying the baby to the window to look outside. So that's what married life was like for a couple who really loved each other. It wasn't all smooth sailing. There were rough spots. But with a little talking, they seemed to be working it through. Surely Maryann and he could do that too.

''All right! Two weeks. But I still think you're trying to gain brownie points with Clay.'' Jordan harrumphed his way out of the room, his footsteps heavy on the parquet flooring Clay had so carefully varnished.

''Uh, you might warn him that refinishing this floor again is going to set him back a few of those computer toys he likes to hoard,'' Clay offered loudly, knowing very well Jordan's office was right next to this room.

The door slammed in response to his remark.

Caitlin grinned. ''Yes!'' she exclaimed exuhltantly. ''I hate cleaning that bathroom. Now, what were we talking about? Oh, yes. The paper.'' She tugged it out, grimaced at the dark smudges on the white leather, then handed the sheaf to Clayton in exchange for Micah.

''What's in here?'' He peered down at the splashy headlines of a paper that was obviously not from Oakburn.

''According to Jordan, the report said something about Amy being there when her father collapsed. Maybe Terrence said something to her before he went into his coma.''

''Said something like what?'' Clay asked absently as he scanned the pages. His eyes halted at the picture of Maryann in front of Wintergreen.

Caitlin was speaking, he knew that. But he didn't

hear a thing she said. His brain was too busy absorbing what the paper said. When he finished, he searched the rest for any other articles, then laid the whole thing down on the table.

"So?"

"It just says Amy and her dad were at a restaurant, and he collapsed. She sat beside him until the paramedics came. Somebody took her to the hospital, and she waited there until her mother showed up. Her father never regained consciousness—according to this, at least."

Caitlin shrugged. "Then I guess only Amy really knows what's bothering her. And she doesn't seem to want to talk about it."

"She will," Clay muttered. "Someday she'll have to deal with it. Just like Maryann." He turned to peer down at Caitlin and gathered up his sketch. "So is this okay with you?"

"Yes, I love it. Especially the way everything is closed in. Less dusting." She grinned.

"She'll probably have me doing that too," Jordan grumbled from the doorway. But there was a softness in his eyes that told Clayton he wouldn't mind a bit.

Micah gurgled, her face wreathed in smiles as her eyes focused on Jordan's face. She held out her arms, and Jordan took her from Caitlin, snuggling the little girl into his shoulder.

"At least someone appreciates me." He glanced up, eyes narrowing as they settled on Clayton.

"We both love you, Jordan. I just don't like newspapers on the sofa." Caitlin stood on tiptoe and kissed his cheek.

"You're going now, right, Clayton?" Jordan's

voice was muffled as his arm snaked around his wife's waist. He clearly wanted a private moment.

"Well, I was asked to stick around for supper..." Clay couldn't resist the tease.

Jordan's head jerked up, his brows lowered fiercely.

Clayton grinned. "But, thanks anyway, I think I'll move on upstairs. There are a few things I need to do at Maryann's. Don't let me interrupt anything."

"We won't!"

"Bye, Clay." Caitlin said. "I'll look forward to the—Jordan!"

Clayton quietly closed the door, his mind full of the love he'd just witnessed. That's what he wanted for himself, he decided. The security of knowing that one special woman loved him more than anyone else in the world. And the pleasure of knowing that no matter what happened, she wouldn't run away from that love.

She's running as hard as she can, the voice inside his head reminded as he climbed the stairs. *You've got yourself a tough row to hoe if you want Maryann MacGregor.*

"Just remember, Lord," Clayton muttered as he knocked on the door, *"good things come to those who wait. And I've waited ten long years. Shouldn't this 'good thing' be mine pretty soon?"*

"Are you talking to yourself?" a familiar voice demanded.

Clayton glanced down to find icy blue eyes glaring at him.

"Only crazy people do that."

He grinned. "It's not the talking to yourself that's the problem, Amy. It's answering your own questions that makes people wonder. Is your mom here?"

"Yes." Amy didn't offer to let him in. "But she's

busy. She has to plan what to wear to her new job tomorrow.''

New job? Maryann? Why would she even dream of working in little old Oakburn? She'd scraped through school by the skin of her teeth, and to his knowledge had never gone to college.

Clayton's eyebrows rose, and his mind went on high alert. What on earth had Maryann gotten herself into now?

Chapter Four

Clay and Maryann had been having the same discussion for ages. For so long, in fact, that Amy had finally taken herself off to play with her dolls after glaring at him for a full five seconds when he'd asked if he could sit down.

"Maryann, you don't *have* to work," he told her again.

"Yes, I do." Her jaw had that stubborn tilt.

"You should be home with Amy."

"Amy needs to get out with other people, become more independent. I need to work to keep my mind alive."

Back and forth, back and forth they went. He'd finally lost his smile, and Maryann wasn't what anyone would term patient.

"This is absolutely none of your business, Clayton Matthews. I'm an adult and I can decide for myself what I want to do. And I want to do this." She snapped the second piece of apple pie down in front of him as if it were a gauntlet, daring him to pick it up.

He did. "Um, this is good. Mare, you haven't been back in town for more than a month. Why the sudden urge to get a job? I know you're not short on cash. And Amy isn't even in school yet, so she could meet the kids some other way. What's the rush?"

"Suddenly you're a financial whiz and a child expert?" she asked. "Well, not that it's any of your business, but Amy is going to a preschool class where she can meet and play with other children. It will be good preparation for kindergarten in the fall. It's not as if I'm going to disappear from her life. I'll be right here. I'm only going to work mornings, to start with."

She sighed, twisting her wedding ring around her finger, her face wistful. "I wish you'd stop trying to take over my life. I know what I'm doing. It's time for me to get out, show people that I'm not the hermit everyone's been saying."

"What about the reporters?" Clay got up from the table and deposited his coffee cup on the counter. Then he screwed a knob onto a new cupboard door with more force than was necessary.

"Most of them have gone now. My story's old news. I imagine it will come up again when the case goes to court, but for now life is pretty peaceful here."

"You don't even know anything about the travel business." He added under his breath, "And I won't be able to stop in there and fix a counter or have a slice of pie." He winced at the frustration he felt.

"Are you kidding, Clay?" She sniffed that elegant nose at him. "I've been to more places than you can imagine. Terrence loved traveling, and before Amy came along we did quite a lot of it."

Aha! Clayton stored that snippet of information away for future dissection. *Before Amy came along*. Meaning that afterward the guy couldn't be bothered, or what?

"I have more firsthand experience about Hawaii, Europe, Australia, England, the Bahamas and a host of other places than most full-fledged travel agents. I've been there, and sometimes I even arranged conferences for Terrence's associates."

It was just another reminder of the differences between them, Clayton mused. He'd never been farther than Minneapolis. And had never wanted to be, either. At least, not until Maryann had left town again after Christmas and he saw all his hopes going down the tubes.

"Anyway, what I don't know, I can learn. And I won't know what I can learn until I try. Leslie said she'd be happy to teach me." She took a sip of her coffee, eyeing the cabinet door he'd just finished hanging. "Besides, I'll be out of your way. You can come in any morning and work by yourself."

Which was exactly what he didn't want.

"The thing is," he muttered, keeping his face averted, "I'm going to be pretty busy for a while. My land has drained, and in a few days I should be able to start seeding. I just thought I'd get these doors hung first."

"Do you do it all yourself?" She nibbled on a crust of pie shell, her eyes curious. "The farming, I mean. It must be difficult."

"It's not that bad." Clayton shrugged, refusing to let her know how lonely it was out there all day long and sometimes well into the night. And how much lonelier it was when he came home to an empty house.

"I've got a system down now and things usually go pretty smoothly."

"Oh."

He could tell she was lost. Maryann had never been particularly interested in farming. It wasn't any wonder her eyes got that fuzzy look when he started babbling about seeders and fertilizer.

"What kind of things does Leslie expect you to do when you don't even know the computer system yet?" Clayton quietly changed the subject. Maryann was right, it really wasn't any of his business what she did.

Leslie Ann Turnbull had started her travel agency five years ago, after retiring from teaching. It had grown by leaps and bounds since then. Residents of Oakburn liked being able to make their travel arrangements locally, and Leslie was good at letting them know when a travel discount was about to be announced.

"I've learned a bit about it already. Yesterday I made a reservation for a flight to California. I just hope I can pick it up quickly enough."

"There's no rush, is there?" He frowned, watching the worry draw tiny lines at the corners of her eyes.

"Sort of. Leslie's got a bus tour to Mexico planned for the first of November. If I can handle it, she'd like me to hold down the fort." He watched her eyes fog over, her mouth working as she chewed her bottom lip.

"That's a long way off. You'll do fine." He tipped up his cup, noticed that the last of the coffee was gone, and knew he had no good reason to hang around any longer. "I'd better go. I've got to pick up some seed this afternoon."

Clay loaded his tools back into his toolbox and set it behind the door while he cleaned up the area. Then he straightened slowly, hating to go but knowing she wouldn't let him stay if there wasn't another job to be done.

"Don't worry about us, Clay. We'll manage just fine." Maryann's wobbly smile firmed up. "We have to."

"You can always count on me, you know that. For anything." He stood there, shuffling from one foot to the other like a nervous stallion, debating whether he should ask about her finances. But no, he wouldn't offer to lend her any money. She didn't need that kind of interference from him. Anyway, she was probably only interested in the job because it would get her out and about.

Finally, when she nodded goodbye, he clapped his hat on his head and tugged open the door. "See you."

"Of course, we'll see you. There's still those closet doors to be done." She raised one eyebrow meaningfully, and Clayton blushed.

"Are you going to the social on Friday night?" he asked, avoiding her eyes.

"I'm not sure. Bingo isn't really my game."

Clay snorted. "It isn't bingo! That went out years ago. Do you really think the pastor would make an announcement from the pulpit for *bingo?*"

"Well, what is it for then? He said bingo." Maryann's dark eyebrows met in a frown of puzzlement. "Is it some kind of code?"

"I guess, though almost everybody knows what it means. There's a surprise shower for Len Toews and Gracie Armstrong. They're getting married in three weeks, and since they both go to our church, we usually hold a couples shower. The pastor was trying to make sure it's a surprise."

Maryann's big blue eyes opened wide as saucers. "You're going to a bridal shower?" she stammered, her lips twitching.

"It's a *couples* shower," he enunciated, feeling the heat rise to his cheeks. "Men and women. Men bring gifts for the groom and women bring gifts for the bride."

He frowned, trying to get a glimpse of her face where she'd hidden it behind her hand. Her shoulders were shaking, and she seemed to be coughing.

"Maryann?" He stood there, wondering what to do next, praying she wasn't crying. He hated crying. His heart sank when he caught sight of the tears rolling down her cheeks between her fingers. Now what?

"I c-can't believe anyone would ever get Clayton Matthews to a bridal shower," she said with laughter, her mouth turned up in a wide grin, "let alone make him walk into Genevieve's Gifts to buy some crystal." The chuckles broke out, ringing around her apartment.

She was laughing at him!

"I don't buy crystal," he informed her testily. "I usually give them something I make. Something for their home."

He stepped through the open doorway, his pride taking an awful beating as he watched the laughter light up her eyes. Happiness gave her skin that luminous glow he remembered from long ago. It was too bad she could only laugh at his expense.

"Perhaps I'll see you there," he murmured. Then he pulled the door closed and walked carefully down the steps, trying to be as quiet as possible so the other inhabitants wouldn't know how long he'd been there—

"Clay?"

He turned back around but kept his eyes on her shoes. Heels, of course, he noticed. As if she wasn't tall enough, Maryann always insisted on wearing heels. He figured it was another of her attempts to show she was as good as the rest of the world. He liked it better when she was short enough to tuck her head against his heart…

"Yes?"

"I'm sorry." She walked down two steps and took his hand. "I didn't mean to laugh. It was just the idea of it that threw me. I've never seen men at bridal showers."

She tried to look penitent, but the corner of her mouth kept twitching, and before long her big wide smile stretched across her face. "I really am sorry. I'm sure it will be a lovely evening."

"You're going?" Hope sprang eternal, Clay mocked himself.

"Sure. Why not? I'll meet you there, shall I? Seven-thirty?"

He sighed. Why was he such a fool for that smile? "Sure. See you there. They have the youth group looking after the kids if you want to bring Amy."

"Okay." She leaned down and touched her lips to his cheek.

Clayton lifted one hand to touch his skin, sure he'd dreamed it. His eyes searched hers.

"I didn't mean to hurt your feelings," she whispered. "I know if you make a gift, it will be wonderful. Thanks for doing the cupboards, friend."

He nodded. "You're welcome. Friend." Hah! He

wanted a whole lot more than a friendship from Maryann MacGregor.

"Bye."

"Bye." His addled brain finally got the message, and he turned, stumbling down the last three stairs and out the door.

He raced down the walk, vaulted over the gate and climbed into his truck with feet like wings. He shifted into reverse before remembering that he had to turn on the motor first.

"Who put that look on your face?" Jordan called from the sidewalk, his face scrunched up into a frown.

Clay leaned out his window, his mouth creasing into a grin he couldn't possibly have stopped.

"Who do you think?" he called back and then took off for home like a scalded rabbit, ready to take on the world.

"She called me 'friend,'" he told his cow Bessie as he milked her twenty minutes later. "That's a start, isn't it?"

Bessie blinked at him once, sloshing her cud around for a better chew, before she turned away. It was obvious the cow had her mind on other matters.

"If I can just get her to realize that we could be more than friends," he muttered, straining the cream as it flowed through the old separator. "Maybe I should start by making her something special." He set the jars of milk and cream in the fridge on the porch, ready for his neighbors to pick up. Then he walked across to his workshop.

"I've already started that dollhouse for Amy for Christmas, but what could I make that's good enough for Maryann?"

He flopped down on a stool and thumbed through an old woodworking catalogue. The center spread was devoted to a jewelry case made of rich ruby mahogany. It had several sliding compartments and two secret ones. It was perfect.

"Her birthday's in August." He thought it over out loud. "That'd give me plenty of time."

It was just enough time. Though he should have been readying the seeder for an early start tomorrow morning, Clay dug through his wood stock, hunting for a particular bit of wood. He found the perfect piece for the lid, an old gnarled burl that would be hard to work. But if he pulled this off, the beauty of the wood would make her eyes pop.

Clay searched the shed for his tool kit, then suddenly leaned back on his heels as he remembered where it was. "She'll think I'm an idiot if I go back tonight," he muttered, feeling his cheeks burn as he remembered that bubbling burst of laughter. "But tomorrow she's going to work. If I go into town in the morning, she'll never know I've been there."

His Maryann wasn't the type to notice tools unless they were in her way, and his were carefully stowed in his toolbox behind the door. *His* Maryann, he liked the sound of that.

"This canvas is gorgeous!" Beth Ainslow twisted her head from side to side, allowing the light to play across the daubs of acrylic that covered the fabric in a wash of bright, eye-piercing splashes. Maryann and Caitlin had gathered in Beth's apartment for a gabfest on Thursday evening, supposedly to help Beth reorganize her cluttered apartment.

"Thank you for the gift, girlfriend. I can't believe

you know how to paint like this. Did you take lessons?'' Beth asked.

"Terrence hired a tutor for me. I'd been dabbling up till then. Remember those graduation sketches I did of you guys?'' Maryann watched for some sign of remembrance.

"I've still got mine!'' Beth rummaged through the box behind the door that she had recently unearthed. "I think it's in here somewhere.''

"You're still a collector, aren't you?'' Caitlin giggled, eyeing the mishmash of things that lay around the apartment. "Your school locker used to look just like this?''

Beth grimaced. "Don't remind me. The store has been keeping me so busy, I haven't had time to do anything lately. Anyone want another coffee?''

"Not me,'' Maryann murmured. "I'll never get to sleep at this rate.'' She smiled at the other two, catching a funny look as it passed between them. "What?''

"I don't think you've been sleeping much at all, have you, Maryann? Last night I heard you walking around at three-thirty.'' Caitlin frowned. "And Beth heard you the night before. Is anything wrong?''

"I'm sorry.'' Maryann flushed. "I didn't realize I'd been making so much noise. I'll really try to be quieter.''

"Don't be silly, Mare. This is your home—make as much noise as you want, for goodness sake. We just wondered if there was something we could help you with.'' Caitlin's face was soft, and her hand reached out to squeeze her friend's. "That's what we're here for, remember?''

"Yep, the Widows of Wintergreen have to stick together.'' Beth snickered as she repeated the slogan they'd all heard around town when they'd first moved into the house. "Except that one of us isn't a widow any longer. Do you think we should ask her to move out?"

"I don't think so." Maryann tossed Caitlin a cheeky look. "Why pay perfectly good money for a baby-sitter when there's one waiting right here?"

"Gee, thanks!" Caitlin rolled her eyes. "Anyway, I don't think it will be long before Maryann joins me in matrimonial bliss. Not if Clayton has anything to say about it. He's crazy about her."

"Still?" Beth sighed. "Ah, young love!"

"She's joking! Anyway, you're one to talk, Bethy. You and Garret still cause sparks when you look at each other," Maryann protested, anxious to take the focus off herself.

"That, my dear, is not love. More like bitterness. Or that monster revenge. From what I've seen, Garret Winthrop would like to wring my neck." Beth pretended a nonchalance that both women knew covered her real feelings of hurt and loss.

"Eliza was over again today." Caitlin broke the extended silence. "My mother-in-law is busy match-making for her daughter. The one, I might add, who does not wish to be matched with anyone. Eliza's arranged a secret meeting for them tonight."

"A secret one?" Maryann frowned. "What does that mean?"

Caitlin shook her head. "Believe me when I say I do not know where this woman gets her ideas from."

"Ooh, sounds juicy!" Beth rubbed her hands together in glee. "Come on, Caity, spill all."

"You know how Natasha loves to play racquetball? Well, Eliza found out Gerald Messer—you know that new single guy who just joined our church—is very sports-minded. Turns out he's really good at racquetball. Anyway, his mother and Eliza are on the same committee at church, and they got talking about it, and Eliza got Mrs. Messer to give her son a birthday gift.''

Beth sighed, glaring at Caitlin. "You're deliberately dragging this out.''

"No, I'm not. But you have to know some of the history to understand what's going on. Anyway…'' She stopped and peered at Maryann. "Are you listening?''

"'Birthday gift,''' Maryann repeated quietly, her gaze riveted on the silent television screen across the room. She sucked in a gasp when Celine Constein's beautiful face flickered into view.

"Maryann? Honey, what's wrong? You're as white as a sheet!'' Beth knelt in front of her, rubbing her friend's hands as she ordered Caitlin to get a glass of water.

Maryann stared at the screen, unable to tear her eyes away from the woman who stood with a baby clutched in her arms. She had stopped it, hadn't she? She'd refused to give Celine a dime. That should be the end of it.

"Honey, what's going on? Why are you so upset? What is it about that woman that makes you so afraid?'' Beth's glance followed hers, her eyes widening as she turned up the sound and heard the accusations. "Maryann, she's claiming that Terrence left her half his estate!''

"I know.''

The picture changed then, flashing to some other earth-shattering event that had happened to someone else halfway round the world.

But Maryann couldn't get the look on that pretty young face out of her mind. The hurt, yes, that was bad enough. But the determination in those eyes! That was something else.

Fear flooded Maryann's soul and she closed her eyes in dismay. Did Celine know about the letter?

"Here, drink this. And then you're going to tell us what it is that's eating you up. It can't be just this alleged affair. We've known about that for weeks now." Caitlin forced her to sip at the ice-cold water, then sank down on a footstool and picked up her hand. "Go ahead, Maryann."

"I don't think I can talk about it." It was ugly, sordid. Not the kind of stuff you shared with your friends.

"Listen, Maryann. We don't care what happened. We just want to help you." Beth glanced at Caitlin, who nodded.

"I told you both how I met Terrence, right? I was waiting tables in a little town. Quite a bit like this one, actually." She smiled, remembering some of the regulars. "It was a truck stop and the men were very decent. All except one. He hassled me every time he came in."

"I know the type," Beth agreed, mouth tight.

"Well, he started needling me, saying things that weren't very nice. I'd pour him coffee, he'd say it was old. I brought his meal, he said it was cold."

"Of course, he ate most of it before he complained, right?" Beth nodded at Maryann's startled look. "I thought so. Sounds exactly like my dad. Nothing I ever did was right. Go on, woman. Talk!"

"Well, when I gave him the bill, he said it wasn't right. He claimed he'd only eaten one piece of pie and even that wasn't fresh. He even claimed there had been a fly in it!''

''And you had no pie left to inspect, I suppose? Typical!''

''He said he'd thrown it out, but that was a lie because I saw him eat both pieces. The place was almost empty by then, and so the manager came out right away to see what was wrong. I tried to explain, but he wouldn't listen. The customer is always right.'' She smiled tiredly, remembering all too vividly how scared she'd been.

''The upshot was, he ordered me to get my coat. I was fired for arguing with a customer.''

''Oh, the creep!'' Caitlin glared at the television, daring it to answer her.

''Just as I was leaving, a man stopped me. He said he wanted me to stay put for a moment. It was Terrence, of course. He called the manager over and handed him a business card. He said I had been wrongfully dismissed, that the trucker had in fact eaten everything and that I hadn't argued with him at all.'' She smiled. ''It felt so nice to finally have someone on my side.''

''What did the manager say?'' Beth asked.

''Nothing! Terrence wouldn't let him speak. He said I would be seeking legal redress and there were plenty of witnesses to back me up. There weren't any that I knew of, but the manager believed Terrence.''

''Hmm. A protector. Nice guy.''

''Yes, he was. I kept my job, even got a raise. Terrence started to stop by now and then for lunch or a coffee. He was doing business in the area. Anyway, we'd chat and sometimes he'd ask me out for dinner after my shift. One day he asked me to marry him. He said he was getting older and he wanted a wife and maybe a family, and that I was exactly what he wanted.''

Maryann risked a look up and saw the knowing looks on their faces. She rushed on with the story. ''I was lonely and scared by then. Nothing had gone the way I'd planned, you see. I didn't have any friends to help me, and Terrence seemed like the answer to my prayers. He said he'd always look after me, that he had more than enough money to support us, that I wouldn't have to wait tables ever again. That was the clincher. I agreed to marry him.''

''Because of the money?'' Beth's usually smiling face was frowning now. ''Honey, you barely knew him.''

''Actually, I knew him quite well by then. And he knew me, knew what I wanted. I wanted to live in a style I was not accustomed to.'' She made a face. ''I know. I was a fool to think it would be so easy.''

The other two said nothing, politely waiting for her to continue.

''I got rid of my ragged jeans and T-shirts. Terrence bought me designer clothes. I took etiquette lessons and learned how to handle myself at the parties he hosted. I learned how to entertain his guests. We traveled, and I learned even more.'' She smiled. ''We got on very well after the first few awkward days.''

''Did you love him?'' Caitlin lifted her baby up and cuddled her close.

''Love didn't have anything to do with our agreement, Caitlin. It was a partnership.'' Maryann sighed. ''I was only nineteen, remember? Everything seemed so wonderful. Terrence was away a lot in the evenings, but that didn't matter. I had so much to learn, so many things to see. My life was everything I'd always wanted, and I gloried in it.''

"So your domestic life was bliss.'' Beth sniffed. "Must be nice.''

"I thought it was. Until I got pregnant.'' She waited for the gasps of dismay.

When nothing happened, she glanced from one to the other. Caitlin sprawled over Beth's sofa, the baby snuggled up on her tummy. Beth sat cross-legged on the floor, yoga style, waiting.

"He didn't want children?''

"Uh, not exactly.'' Maryann winced, but decided to say it anyway. Maybe then they'd drop the issue. "He didn't want me to be pregnant. I think he wanted to adopt or something. Anyway, he was furious.''

"But he got over it. Right?'' Caitlin's earnest face dared her to deny it.

"After a while.''

"How long after?''

"I don't really want to go into that. It's painful for me. I've never told anyone else this.'' Maryann felt the blush stain her cheeks and kept her eyes down.

Caitlin sat up so fast that the baby squawked. "There's nothing for you to be ashamed of. Anyway, from what Amy says, her father loved her.''

"Yes, he did. He bonded with Amy right after she was born.''

"She was Daddy's pet. That's why she's always talking about 'my daddy,' isn't it?'' Beth asked.

Maryann nodded.

"So everything worked out fine. Right?'' Beth's eyes were narrowed, thoughtful.

"I suppose it did,'' she agreed quietly.

"So what is it about this woman that makes you

blanch as if you'd seen a ghost?'' Caitlin still frowned, her forehead pleated in puzzlement.

It was obvious to Maryann that she couldn't tell them the truth, not if she expected them to stay her friends.

"Sweetie, did your Terrence actually have an affair with that woman? Is that the problem?''

Shocked that they'd verbalized what she'd kept so carefully hidden all these weeks, Maryann could only stare mutely at Beth and nod.

"You're afraid this baby on television is his, is that it?''

Maryann nodded again.

"But Amy is five. That kid is no more than ten or eleven months old— Oh, I see.'' Beth was obviously confused by this new thought.

She'd let them think it was only the once, Maryann decided, trying to rescue her mind from the foggy state into which it had fallen.

"Even if it is his child, it can't hurt you, Maryann. You're okay, aren't you?'' Caitlin shifted from one foot to the other, jiggling the baby to quiet her, eyes dark with turmoil. "I mean, he died a while ago. The estate has already been settled. They have no claim on anything.''

"It can hurt Amy.'' Maryann swallowed, knowing her concern wasn't only for her child. "She adored Terrence. He lavished toys and gifts on her as if she were a little princess. He even had a special telephone line hooked up to his office so she could talk to him whenever she wanted. He wouldn't have wanted her hurt by this.'' On the other hand, he wasn't there to put her to bed or kiss her good-night most of the time, but she wouldn't tell them that.

"In time this woman might accept it, Maryann."

Caitlin frowned. "She hasn't got time, Beth. The way they're plastering this stuff over the TV, Amy could turn the thing on and hear it all."

"Terrence always called Amy his 'best girl.' That baby is a girl. Can you imagine what that would do to Amy if she learned, at this stage, that her daddy had another little girl? That she wasn't his only daughter, that *special* little girl he always claimed?" She shook her head. "I can't allow that. She's fixated on the idea of family, and this would confuse her terribly."

"And that's why you came back here? To get away from the stigma of this other child." Beth nodded. "I knew there had to be another reason."

"There was," Maryann told her softly, swallowing. "I wanted to make a new life for us. I thought if I left, this woman would forget about suing me, that the media attention would die down and we could live a normal life. I thought I could go back to being me— plain old Maryann."

Beth snorted, pointing to Maryann's silk pants and angora sweater.

"Darlin', you could never be called 'plain.' Not with those eyes and that hair. You should have gone in for modeling, not settled for old Terrence."

"Terrence gave me exactly what I asked for." Maryann smiled sadly. "Money, prestige, a name. I can't complain if everything didn't go exactly as I expected."

A long silence hung in the room as they each considered the hopes and dreams they'd thought so easy to achieve ten years ago.

"What will you do now?" Caitlin asked quietly.

"That's the big question, isn't it?" Maryann shrugged, clicking the remote so the screen went black. "I haven't got anywhere else to go, and even if I did, Amy's just starting to fit in around here. I don't want to move her again."

"What about the rest of your family?" Beth's eyes were soft with compassion. "Wouldn't they help?"

"I can't go running to them with my problems. My sisters have their own problems and my brother is in the navy. Anyway, I couldn't ask them. I have to deal with this myself."

They were staring at her, feeling sorry for her. She wouldn't allow that. She didn't need anyone's pity.

"Those pictures of that child are bound to bring the reporters around again," Caitlin murmured thoughtfully.

"I can deal with them. They never print the truth, anyway." Because they don't know the truth, she thought. If they did, you'd be in even more hot water.

"Listen, Mare, I don't want to be nosy, but are you okay for money?"

"I'm fine."

"Maybe if you offered a settlement?"

"It's not that easy, Beth. She's asking for the estate to be split between Amy and her daughter," Caitlin murmured, then offered Maryann a half mile of apology.

So her friends had been following the case? So much for keeping things private.

"Maryann, honey, your Terrence didn't leave you strapped, did he?" Beth's earnest face peered into hers.

"Not strapped, no."

"But not wealthy either," Caitlin guessed.

"I'm not broke, though. Don't think that! And Amy has her college fund tucked safely away in a trust. It's just that there wasn't a whole lot left over once I paid what we owed, though I expect it would seem a fortune to some people." Maryann couldn't help glancing at the blank television screen.

"We lived very well, you see. I liked to buy nice things, and Terrence seemed to enjoy having them too. I thought we could afford it, and I guess I never paid much thought to the future. I never really knew what our income and expenses were. Terrence handled all of that."

"I could lend you some cash, if you need it. Just between us two. No strings." Caitlin kept her gaze on the baby.

They were so dear, Maryann thought, tears welling. She didn't even have to ask, and there they were offering help.

"Thank you, but no, Caitlin. I'm fine. Amy and I have enough to live quite comfortably. I'd like to give this Miss Constein something, if only for the sake of her child, even if it isn't Terrence's. But I can't. I have to watch out for my daughter."

And yourself, her conscience mocked her nastily. *Anyway, 'some' money isn't what your husband wanted Celine to have.* She deliberately shut out the voice.

"My idea is probably against all legal advice," Beth muttered, pouring herself another cup of coffee. "Don't lawyers always say that you open the door with one altruistic move?"

"Yes, they do. They've warned me that if I give her a dime, she'll just keep coming back." It sounded horrible, Maryann mused sadly, as if she begrudged the poor woman enough to feed her daughter and herself. "I'd better go. Amy will be coming home from that birthday party soon."

"And Jordan will be pacing." Caitlin picked up the baby and kissed the top of her head. "He thinks it's his right to put Micah down each night."

"That's wonderful! I wish my dad had thought like that. He figured it was his right to rant and rave, and our obligation to listen to him." Beth hugged her friend and waited a moment as mother and daughter crossed the hall.

Then she turned back to Maryann, a quizzical look on her face. "You're sure that's all that's bothering you, Mare? There's nothing else?"

Maryann's hand, which was stretched out holding a sofa cushion, froze midair as she searched that small piquant face. "W-what do you mean, Beth?" she breathed.

"It's just that you seem so..." The petite woman shrugged. "I don't know how to put it. It's as if you have to make a decision, and you're torn between the choices available."

Maryann gulped, amazed at how close Beth had come to the truth. Of course, there really wasn't any choice. Not when you looked at it in the cold hard light of day. She was a mother, with a daughter. They were used to living in a certain style, to having what they wanted. She couldn't just give away their future.

Could she? It wasn't just pure selfishness, was it?

"You're sure there's nothing Caitlin or I can do, other than pray for you? We'd like to help out, and I know you've been losing sleep over this. Maybe if you told Clay, he could think of something..."

Not Clay, her brain screamed. *Not dear, sweet, trusting Clay.*

"That's so sweet of you, but no. Thanks anyway, Beth. I'll just have to deal with it in my own way." She folded the afghan the baby had been lying on and set it aside. "I'd better go."

Beth walked her to the door. "Don't worry about it, okay, Mare? Just give it all to the Lord and let Him deal with it. There's a way through, and you'll find it. Trust in Him."

"I'll, uh, try," Maryann blathered, keeping her eyes averted. "I'm sure everything will be just fine. God will take care of us."

"That's the spirit."

She returned Beth's boisterous hug and then left, pulling the apartment door behind her with relief. All the way up the stairs she could hear the voice pounding in her ears.

Liar! Cheat. Thief.

"Stop it," she hissed, racing inside her apartment and slamming the door shut. "Just stop it."

"To him who knows right and does it not, to him it is sin."

"I can't. Don't you understand? I can't throw everything away now. How would we live? What would happen to my daughter?"

"Trust in the Lord with all your heart and don't lean to your own understanding."

"But what would I do? How would we ever manage?"

"In all your ways acknowledge Him, and He will direct your paths."

The words rolled round and round, turning her brain into an aching pile of mush.

"I can't just walk away from that money. I can't!"

"Mommy?" Amy's solemn face peered up at her, denim hat slightly askew. "What's the matter? What's wrong, Mommy?"

"Nothing, my darling. Nothing at all. I didn't hear you come in." Maryann forced a smile to her lips as she hugged the little girl. "Did you enjoy the party?"

But as she caught a glimpse of her own reflection in the mirror, clutching her daughter, Maryann couldn't hide the truth from her own knowing eyes.

She was wrong and she knew it. The problem was, she couldn't do anything about it. Not tonight, not tomorrow.

Not ever, if she wanted to keep her daughter.

What would Clay think if she told him she was going to deny Terrence's illegitimate daughter her rightful inheritance so that she could keep her own life intact?

Chapter Five

"**I** need to apologize, Clay." Maryann stood before him in the center of the church's fellowship hall, her face troubled.

"For what?" He frowned, trying to figure out this latest change in Maryann.

"For being really rude the other day. I had no right to mock you about getting a shower gift. Yours was the best gift here." She slid one hand down the glossy patina of a square flour canister that sat nestled beside four smaller matching containers.

"Forget it." He brushed it off. "I thought you were teasing anyway."

"I was, but not in a nice way. I'm sorry I didn't realize earlier that you did such wonderful things with wood, though I have enough hints in my apartment, don't I?" She rolled her eyes. "Those oak canisters are the most beautiful ones I've ever seen."

"Thank you." He studied her face, noting the cheekbones that protruded just a little more than they had last week. "How are you?"

"I'm fine. They certainly seemed to enjoy tonight. It must be hard for a young couple to think about a shower just days before their wedding."

"Doesn't look like it bothers them too much." Clay grinned, chuckling as the groom turned an adoring look on the crystal dish his fiancée was showing him. "They can hardly wait to get married."

"I see that," Maryann murmured, her gaze intent on the loving couple. "It must be nice."

"Surely you know what it's like? You were married."

"Yes, I was. But we didn't have all the pre-wedding celebration. Just a ceremony at city hall. It wasn't the same as this at all." She motioned around her. "They've planned every detail, thought things through, waited for five months, Caitlin said. What could go wrong now?"

Clay thought about that while Maryann busied herself packing and folding the multitude of tea towels, bathroom towels and other assorted linens into the boxes provided. By the looks of it, the happy couple wouldn't need to go shopping for a while.

"I guess there's always something that can go wrong in any marriage," he mumbled, refusing to budge from her side. "The only thing you can do is love each other enough to forgive, come to some kind of compromise and move on. If two people love each other, they'll strive to work it out."

"Maybe."

She sounded unsure of that, and Clay couldn't help but wonder again what her marriage had been like. It didn't sound as though there had been much love.

"How's the job?"

"It's wonderful," she replied enthusiastically, turning to him with an armload of blankets. "I've never enjoyed anything as much as working at the travel agency. Each day is a new experience, and Leslie is a sweetheart. Yesterday I booked Mr. and Mrs. Armitage a trip to San Francisco. Do you know it's their twenty-fifth anniversary in August?"

"Their kids are going to have a party for them. But don't say anything 'cause it's going to be a surprise." He saw the faraway look float into her vivid eyes.

"Twenty-five years is a long time, isn't it? And yet George says it seems like yesterday. I can't imagine being married to someone for twenty-five years."

"Mommy!" Amy's strident voice cut across the roomful of chitchat. "Come here, Mommy!" She stood defiant as a sitter gave up coaxing her to return to the playroom in the corner.

"Maryann, can you help me wrap some of these dishes? I don't want anything to get broken, and I'm sure you're far better at packing than I," the pastor's wife called.

As Clay watched, Maryann glanced helplessly from her daughter's imperious face across the room, to the pastor's wife. There was clearly nothing wrong with Amy, but Clay didn't like her tone of voice—Maryann wasn't a servant whose presence should be demanded.

"Now, Mommy!"

On the other hand, she *was* the child's mother. And Maryann no doubt wanted to placate her daughter, to make sure everything was all right. Which was exactly what the little miss wanted, he decided, and then chided himself for being jealous of a child. Clay figured he'd better help out.

"I'll see what Amy wants. You deal with the gifts. I can't pack to save my life. Okay?" Clay waited for

Maryann's nod. Once received, he patted her arm and then started off across the room to the spot where Amy stood, hands on her hips, her eyes shooting daggers at him.

"Where is my mom?" It was not what she meant, and Clay knew it. When she called, she expected her mother to answer, *now*.

"She's talking to someone right now, Amy. Is there something I can help you with? Aren't you supposed to be with the other children?"

"No." Amy thrust her chin in the air and stood where she was, waiting for his next coaxing words.

Clay smiled. "Oh. Okay then, if you're sure. Only don't call out again like that because it disrupts the party. There are no children allowed in here, you see."

"Why?"

He could see she hated asking it. "Because this is a wedding shower for adults. That couple over there are getting married. Everyone here wants all the focus and attention on them. This is their special occasion."

"Why?" More quiet now, less arrogant.

"Well, people usually only get married once and they like to have lots of happy memories of that time to remember later. Do you know what memories are?"

"Yes."

"And I guess you've got some good ones too, haven't you?" He waited for her to nod while he hooked a chair nearer and sank down into it so that they were huddled together.

"Yes," the little girl finally agreed. Her black felt hat hung over one eye and she jerked it back in place, her face a mixture of emotions. "Most of them are good."

"Most people have both kinds of memories," he

told her softly. "Good ones are nice to keep so you can think about them, and bad ones are nice to get rid of."

"You have good memories?" Amy's pert little nose wrinkled up in disbelief. "Like what? Silly old farming, I suppose?"

"Some of my good memories are from the farm, yes." He nodded.

"Tell me."

It was not a request. Clayton pretended he was daydreaming, his eyes fixed on the plain and definitely ordinary fluorescent fixtures that hung from the ceiling.

"Would you please tell me about your memories?" Amy amended after several moments, her tone less angry, though still full of suspicion.

"Well, there are the memories I have of the baby chicks we used to get in the spring, when I was a kid. Little soft fuzzy balls of yellow fluff that you could hold in your hand." She looked interested in that. "I just got another batch yesterday."

"I want to hold one."

"Maybe one day," he said. "I have a good memory of laying in the field in the middle of summer, when the grain was very high and no one could find me. I was hidden there, and I could look up in the sky and watch the clouds pass by. I liked that."

"Were you lost?"

The child looked worried by that, and Clay figured she was a little too young to understand such pleasures. Either that or you had to be there. He wasn't sure which.

"You know what my very best memory is?" He

thought a moment and then amended that. "Well, my second best memory?"

"No."

Her eyes were every bit as wide as Maryann's and in that moment, Clay could see her mother at this same age. He smiled and carefully brushed his hand over the fragile blond ringlets that tumbled around her head.

"Well? Tell me. Now!"

He looked at her sadly. "Don't speak like that, Amy. It's rude."

"Now!" she ordered, voice rising.

Clay shook his head, refusing to cow to her temper. "No. You're not being very nice, and I don't want to talk about it anymore."

"I want to know." She slapped her hands on her hips.

He shook his head, his mind made up. She wasn't going to get away with ordering him around. "Nope. Not here. Besides, I don't want anyone to hear."

"Why?"

"Because it's a secret that I only share with very special friends. I thought you and I were friends, but friends don't talk to each other like that."

"That's not fair!" She stomped her foot in anger. "You said you'd tell me. Tell me!" Her face was beet-red with temper, her tiny hands clenched at her sides.

Clay opened his eyes wide at the sight. "I've already said no, Amy. Stop acting like this."

"Say it," she hissed, her angry face now mere inches from his. "You promised, now say it!"

He shook his head.

"I'm telling my mom." She whirled around as if

to leave, and then noticed that he wasn't following. "Don't you care? You'll get in trouble with her."

"But then you won't know the memory, will you, Amy?" he told her softly. "You see, life doesn't work like that. You can't make someone do something by bullying them. No one wants to be ordered around or yelled at. Friends are nice to one another."

"You're not my friend." Scorn laced her voice.

"I'd like to be. But friends don't boss friends and act rudely. Friends—real friends—consider the other person's feelings."

She bit her lip, her eyes narrowing. "You don't know anything. My dad yelled at my mommy sometimes. She didn't care." The blue eyes waited for his reaction.

Keep calm, Clay ordered his fuming brain. *Amy has eyes and ears that hear more than a lot of kids.*

He felt totally mystified by this small bundle of femininity. She was laughing one moment, bristling with fury the next. What did he know about dealing with any of that?

And yet, if he ever got the chance to marry Maryann, Amy, with all her baggage, memories and history, would be part of that marriage. He froze at the very idea of being a father. What did he know about fathering? A man whose father had run away rather than face up to his responsibilities to a wife and six kids.

"I think your mommy cared, Amy. I think she cared very much. I'll bet that deep inside it hurt really bad when your dad yelled at her. I know it hurts her when you do it."

She thought about that for a while, her face wrinkled with puzzlement. "My mom loves me." She sounded faintly uncertain.

"Of course she does." He let that sink in for a moment. "But the question is, do you love her? I think you do. But I also think you haven't been showing her very much love when you act nasty like you just did. I don't think that child is the real true Amy."

"My dad said I was his most special girl. You don't know anything." The clenched jaw and jutting chin told him she didn't appreciate his comments. "We're a fam'ly. Are you gonna tell me the memory or not?"

He shook his head. "Not tonight. Maybe some other time, when you're old enough to act politely."

"I'm old enough now." Again she stomped her foot in frustration.

Clay just widened his eyes, stared at her foot and then shifted his stare to her red face. "Really?"

"Ooh!" Amy turned and marched toward the children's play area. Then she stopped and came back, her eyes glittering with rage. "I didn't want to know about your stupid old memory anyhow. I hate you!"

"I'm sorry about that. Maybe another time, then. When we can be friends again." He turned and walked away, leaving her standing there.

Clay picked up the streamers, gathered up used paper cups and napkins, and generally made himself useful until Maryann was finished packing up the gifts. But from the corner of his eye he watched as Amy finally returned to the playroom, head down, a frown marring her pretty mouth. And all the while he reproached himself for his set-to with her—a five-year-old child!

What kind of man dangles a carrot over a little girl and then refuses to give it to her because she's acting up? Amy wasn't his daughter to teach, and he had no business trying to get her to alter her attitude. He had no idea how one handled a five-year-old girl who'd lost her father and needed to prove that her mother would always be there if she needed her. He might have damaged her psyche or something.

"What did Amy want?" Maryann stood holding a punch bowl, her face curious.

"Oh." He flushed. "I don't know. We never got around to that. Sorry."

She shrugged. "It doesn't matter. Obviously it wasn't important."

"Are you almost finished?"

"Just about. I think this is the last gift. Why?"

"Just thought I'd walk you home. I'm about ready to leave myself." He shuffled his garbage bag to the other side. "If you don't mind, that is?"

"Of course I don't mind! Just give me five minutes."

She was as prompt as she was beautiful, and Clayton couldn't help feeling proud as he walked with her toward Wintergreen. He smiled, noting that Amy kept her distance on the other side of her mother, ignoring him as if he had leprosy.

"How is your seeding going?" Maryann asked.

"Actually, very well. That's why I was able to get to the shower. I've almost finished and it was easier to take tonight off after that rain this afternoon." Also, he'd wanted to see her again, but he didn't mention that.

"Is it hard to decide which crops to plant?" She frowned. "I hate making decisions. I always make the wrong ones."

"No, it's not that hard. I pray about it, of course. And check the prices and then I decide. Once the seed's in the ground, I'm committed. From there on it's up to God.''

Maryann seemed to puzzle over that.

"There's no way I could ever unplant all those seeds, so whatever is sown is what I'll get," he explained. "That's why you do a lot of research first. Once you're committed, there's no going back."

The words seemed to shake her. Clay saw her cheeks whiten and felt her hand tighten on his arm. She said nothing more until they got to her front door.

"Thanks for walking us home, Clay. And for helping out tonight. I know they appreciated it."

"The same could be said of you," he grinned. "I guess that's what small towns are all about, helping where you can." He glanced down at the little girl. "Good night, Amy."

Amy sniffed and stomped up the stairs.

"Amy?" Maryann's voice was firm and brooked no argument.

A huge sigh left the little chest, but eventually the dainty feet turned around, marched down the steps and stopped. One hand was thrust out toward him in an exaggerated motion.

"Good night, Mr. Matthews."

He shook it carefully, a smile twitching at the corners of his mouth. "Good night, Amy. Have sweet dreams."

She sniffed, then bounded up the stairs, her shoes thudding up to the third story.

"Good night, Clay. Thanks for everything." Maryann smiled down at him from the second step. As usual she wore heels, and standing on the step she was taller than he.

She held out her hand, and he took it, then tugged

her forward just the slightest bit. He caught her as she came toward him and brushed his lips across her cheek in the most forthright gesture he'd ever made to Maryann MacGregor.

"Clayton!" She stared at him, her cheeks flushed.

"Yes?" He made himself stand where he was. According to Jordan, if you wanted something, you had to go after it.

Maryann stared into his eyes for several moments before her arms crept up around his neck. "That wasn't a good-night kiss."

"It wasn't?" His knees shook like rubber as he slowly interpreted her smile.

"Uh-uh. This is." And with a trill of laughter she leaned closer and placed her lips on his.

Clay stood transfixed for about five seconds, then woke up and took full advantage of the situation.

"How about that?" he asked.

"*That* was a good-night kiss," she reassured him, touching her lips with one finger. She removed her arms and pulled away from him, preceding him to the foyer door. "Good night, Clay."

"Good night, Maryann."

She watched him walk away, his long lean legs stretching in powerful strides down the walkway. To catch a last glimpse of him walking back to the church, she had to follow him partway down the walk.

"He kissed me," she whispered to herself, turning to go inside. "He really and truly kissed me."

"I know. And he did a pretty good job of it too." Beth giggled from behind her.

"He was just being a friend." Maryann climbed the steps and walked inside the foyer, aware that Beth had followed and closed the outside door behind her. "It wasn't anything to get all worked up about."

"It looked pretty friendly to me too," Caitlin murmured, Micah nestled on one hip. "And you didn't seem to be protesting."

Maryann marched toward the stairs, embarrassed by their smug looks.

"It was just a good-night kiss," she mumbled, climbing as quickly as she could.

Reaching the doorway, she called out, "Come on, Amy. Let's get you to bed."

"Can you read me *Cinderella?*"

Maryann ignored the giggles from below as she closed the door firmly on her friends. "We had *Cinderella* last night. And the night before. What about *Sleeping Beauty?*"

"I want *Cinderella.*" The frown on Amy's face challenged Maryann and, giving in to the intuition that told her to get the tired child to bed, she caved without even arguing.

Ten minutes later, the glass slipper had been returned to its wearer, Amy muttered, "Cinderella's daddy shouldn't got her a new mom. Her new mom was mean." Her eyes were half closed, and she yawned and snuggled her hands under one cheek. "He was silly to do that."

Maryann didn't argue. There was no point. Amy was asleep seconds later. Still, it was a curious thought for the child, and she puzzled over it for a few minutes before shrugging. She flicked off the light and moved down the hallway to the window that looked out over the backyard.

Below, in the old creaking swing, Caitlin and Jordan sat snuggled together, whispering and giggling like a couple of teenagers. The sight made Maryann's stomach clench.

Why couldn't she have had that kind of marriage? Why hadn't God made Terrence love her?

Because you didn't love him, her conscience reminded. *You loved his money and what it could buy for you. You still do.*

Maryann winced as the truth of those words hit home.

"It's not really true," she whispered. "I don't love money. But I have to think of my daughter and our future, don't I?"

Mentally she divided the amount from Terrence's estate in half and then divided it by the fifteen or so years Amy would be living at home until college. The number was the same as the last three times she'd done the math. Paltry.

"We couldn't manage on that!" She gulped. "Not even if I worked full-time."

She wanted so much for Amy. Ballet and music lessons. A chance to try out for the swim team. School holidays at camp, and travel that included exciting trips overseas. Maybe a year as an exchange student. Things she herself had longed for and never received. And she wanted to be home with Amy as much as possible.

"It's not my fault," she murmured, watching as her friends shared a kiss in the rose garden and then ambled inside. "I didn't create this situation!"

No, it wasn't her fault. She hadn't wanted any of this. But how was she supposed to deal with what she'd been given?

And where did Clayton Matthews come into it? Could she go on seeing him, allowing him to kiss her, to think they had a future together, while she concealed this letter and did nothing to fulfill Terrence's last wish?

Why me, God? She prayed silently, tears coursing down her cheeks. *Why did You have to spoil it all? Terrence is gone. Clay and I could be together, and I wouldn't have to worry all the time about making ends meet. We'd be happy, I know we would.*

But one question haunted her. Would she be happy living a lie?

Chapter Six

"Oh, no! Not again." Maryann groaned under her breath as she spied Clay stride through the travel agency door for the third time in as many hours. He'd been coming in for weeks now, ever since he'd finished seeding.

"The Hawaiian Islands are a wonderful place to get away in the winter," she babbled to the couple seated across from her. She glanced up through her lashes to follow Clay's progress. Thankfully he'd stopped to look at a brochure.

"Of course, it's too early to book yet, and I don't suppose you want to go in June anyway, but a good look through these pamphlets should give you an idea of what you have to look forward to next winter." She handed over the pamphlets.

"We like to be organized, don't we, Hortense?" John Hilton gathered the folders up and carefully placed them inside his briefcase.

"We do. We certainly do. Thank you, my dear."

"You're more than welcome. Come again, anytime." Maryann waited until the elderly couple were out the door, and then moved toward the tall gentlemen who stood in front of the Alaska brochures.

"I believe you were next?"

"No, I was. Peter's just looking. Right, Pete?" Clayton's voice deepened meaningfully on the last two words, his eyebrows drawn together in a frown.

"I guess I can wait." Good old Pete blinked twice and then went back to his blank perusal of the brochures.

"Good." Clay grinned. "Maybe Leslie will be able to help you soon."

"Clayton Matthews, what are you doing here again?" Maryann sputtered, cheeks heating as the assorted male patrons gathered in the agency observed him toss his arm so nonchalantly around her waist.

"This is the third time this morning, Clay. What do you want?" She kept her voice low, her smile firmly in place so no one would guess the turmoil he'd caused.

"I brought you something." He held out a cup from the local diner. "It's cappuccino."

"Thank you. That was very thoughtful. But it's almost noon. I don't really need something to drink right now."

Just as she hadn't really wanted the cinnamon danish he'd delivered just after the shop opened. Or the chocolate bar he'd delivered an hour later.

"What are you really doing here, Clay?"

"Seeing you."

It wasn't what she'd expected him to say, and she swallowed, trying to put her next question politely. "Why?"

"Because I want to be with you."

He said it so matter-of-factly that a full minute elapsed before Maryann actually absorbed the meaning.

"Clay!" She was fully aware of the seven sets of ears now eagerly listening in on their conversation.

His eyes were dark with emotion. "It's true."

"Yes, but you don't tell someone that in the middle of their workday, with a crowd around. And besides, I can't be with you."

"How do you know? You haven't even tried." He was as angry as she, his face set in a determined frown. "If you'd give me a chance, you'd see that I'm not just a dumb farmer, or as much of an oaf as you think."

"Clayton Matthews, I never, ever, said you were dumb or an oaf." She moved to stand in front of him, hands on her hips. "Did I?"

"That was the impression I got," he muttered, his lips pursed.

"You two should really discuss this somewhere else," Leslie murmured, her voice soft and full of amusement as she moved to stand beside them. "Why don't you take an early lunch, Maryann? You can come back after, if you want."

"Thank you, Leslie. I appreciate it. I'll get this straightened out right away." Maryann grabbed her purse and Clayton's arm, and dragged him past the grinning onlookers and onto the street.

He followed meekly behind, his steps loud on the sidewalk. Maryann was embarrassingly conscious of the shopkeepers who stood at their windows, peering out at them. Gossiping, no doubt. As if she needed any more of that!

Stoicly she made her way down the length of the

main street until finally they came to the corner. One block further and they were at Wintergreen. Maryann strode up the stairs and pulled him inside the entry.

"All right, Clay. What are you trying to do to me?"

"Hi, Maryann. Clay." Jordan glanced from one to the other, juggling a stack of papers in his arms as he closed the front door. "Everything okay?"

"Oh, just peachy, thanks, Jordan. Clay here has made me a total laughingstock in front of the whole town now that the reporters have finally left me alone. But, hey, other than that, I'm great!"

"All right, then." Jordan quickly opened the door to his own apartment, his eyes fixed at the floor. "I'll, uh, see you both later. Or not. Whatever." He slipped inside without a backward look, the door closing quietly behind him.

"Ooh!" She clenched her teeth. "We can't talk here. Let's go." She led the way up the stairs, thankful that Clay followed without a protest.

Inside the apartment Maryann flung her purse on the sofa, held out a chair and motioned him into it. "Sit. And I'm warning you, this better be good."

"It can't be that much of a surprise to you, Maryann. I've been crazy for you for years."

"Oh, Clayton!" She sighed, her head whirling with the knowledge that he'd actually said it. Twice. "Don't you think you might be exaggerating just a little bit? You don't even know me." She lowered her voice. "Not really."

"I'm not a kid anymore, Maryann. I know what I feel. I've known it for a long time. I want to marry you. Is that so terrible?"

Maryann gasped. "Marry me? But...but I can't! I

mean, I've been married, Clay, and I didn't do a very good job of it.''

"So you'll do better this time.''

How could he sound so sure?

Because he knows nothing about your dirty little secret, an inner voice mocked. *He'd change his mind fast if he understood how badly you're clinging to that money. Nobody wants to have a gold digger for a wife.*

She thrust the ugly words away. She wasn't a bad person. She just needed a little security, something behind her so she'd know she could care for Amy.

"Clay, try to understand,'' she began, intent on making him see her side of things. "I'm glad you're my friend. And I'm glad I came back to Oakburn.''

"Me too.'' He tipped back in his chair, hands clasped behind his head. "This way we can really get to know each other before we get married.''

"You're not listening.'' She lowered her voice, conscious of the rest of the residents of Wintergreen. She sighed. "I am not marrying you. Some days I don't even like you!''

"You'll probably grow to like me,'' he murmured, his eyes half closed. "Most people do, once they get to see the real me.''

"What's the real you?'' She was put out by his calm acceptance of her denial.

"You know the real me, Maryann. What you're lacking is the details. I can supply those.'' He sat up straight, tossed his cap onto the coatrack. "For instance, I'm not always going to be a farmer, you know. I'm thinking of doing something different.''

"You are?'' She could hardly imagine it. Clay Matthews *not* on a farm?

"I am.'' He nodded as if to emphasize his decision.

"I'm thinking of renting the farm out after I take this crop off in a couple of months. I have enough to pay the rent on the Phipps' building downtown, and I can display some of my stuff there."

"Your 'stuff'?" she repeated, confused by this new side of him. "What stuff?"

"Oh, that's right. You've never seen the bigger pieces I make. Come on." Clay surged to his feet, grabbed her hand and tugged her toward the door, snagging his cap on the way.

"What are you doing? I have to go get Amy in ten minutes." Maryann took her purse from him, watched him lock her door and then followed him down the stairs, her mind reeling. "Clayton, what is all this about?"

"I'm taking you to the farm. I have something to show you. I'm going to prove that I can be more than just a farmer. We'll pick up Amy on the way." He yanked the outside door closed with a slam, his hand never releasing hers.

"Wait a minute!" Maryann stood her ground. "I haven't had lunch and neither has Amy. Besides, how do you know I have time to go to the farm? I'm supposed to go back to work, remember?"

"She said if you *wanted* to." Clay didn't look worried. "You can make the time up another day. And we'll stop for lunch on the way." He tugged once more. "Come on, Maryann."

"You are so bossy," she muttered, but she followed just the same. Curiosity impelled her to walk toward his truck. What kind of a man was this Clayton Matthews? She'd always assumed he loved farming, that woodworking was just a hobby. Now he was going to turn it into a business?

When they drove into the parking lot at the day care a few minutes later, Amy was racing around the playground. With the arrival of summer holidays, the preschool had closed. Fortunately for Maryann, her daughter loved playing with the other children, and she was only too willing to spend a few hours each morning with her friends at the cooperative.

"What's *he* doing here?" Amy demanded loudly when Clay opened the door for her mother to get out.

"Mr. Matthews has invited us for lunch."

Maryann collected her daughter's backpack, straightened her ever-lopsided hat, and then folded the smaller hand in her own. She hoped her confidence overrode her own nervousness.

"What kind of lunch?" Amy displayed a true five-year-old's pickiness. "Are we having hamburgers?"

"If you want." Clay made sure the little girl was fastened in the seat behind, stowed her backpack beside her, then helped Maryann back inside his truck. "I'd rather have chicken nuggets."

"Do they have sweet an' sour sauce?" Amy's forehead puckered in a frown of intense concentration. "I don't like 'em unless they have the right sauce."

"I'm not sure. We can ask." Clay slowed so the Carruthers sisters could pull out into traffic. The ancient sedan dawdled along at a sedate fifteen miles an hour.

Maryann noticed that he didn't ride their bumper, nor did he attempt to pass their lumbering vehicle. It took patience to follow along, one foot hovering over the brake, as the sisters' car swayed all over the road. She admired his calmness when the old girls finally decided to turn left after signaling right. Once they were safely out of traffic, he stepped up the pace.

"We had a puppet show today," Amy volunteered from the back. "It was *Cinderella.*"

Maryann stifled a groan. What was the fascination with this story? "Did you like it?"

"Uh-huh. 'Cept the part about the ugly stepsisters. I never like that part. Cinderella's dad was silly. He already had a little girl. He didn't need a new fam'ly."

Maryann winced, remembering a little girl still back in New York whose father was also Amy's.

"He probably had lots of love to go around for all of them," Clay murmured, checking the side mirror as he pulled up in front of the local fast-food place.

"She was s'posed to be his special girl. You can't have two specials." Amy's disparaging tone told them exactly what she thought of that idea.

Apparently Clay wasn't defeated. "Why not?" he demanded. "I've got lots of favorite foods. And way more than one special person in my life. There's your mom, and you, and Micah and Pastor Willoughby. And that's only a few." He helped her out, lifting her down from the high cab.

"But they're not the most-specialest ones," Amy said scornfully. "You can only have one most-specialest."

"Really?" Clay looked confused for a moment. "I wonder how God does it then?"

Maryann climbed down unaided, well aware that her daughter and Clay were squaring off for a battle. Amy had that glint of anger in her eyes. She stood facing him down, her feet spread a little apart.

"How God does what?" Amy demanded, swatting her hat back on.

"Loves more than one person at a time." He held out a hand, closing his fingers tightly around Maryann's. "Mare, do you think God loved His son more than He does us?"

"I don't think so."

"I do." Amy glared at their clasped hands, her mouth tightening into a hard line. She walked forward and pushed herself between them, grabbing onto her mother with one hand, and finally, after much contemplation, taking Clay's in her other. It was obvious she meant to prevent him from touching Maryann.

"But Amy, darlin', the Bible says that God *is* love. If pepper is pepper, it can't run out of pepper, can it?"

She blinked at him. "Huh?"

Clay laughed as he bent down and scooped up a handful of gravel from the parking lot.

"Which part of this isn't gravel?"

Amy studied the stones carefully. "It's all gravel," she muttered finally.

"Right! Now pretend that this handful of gravel is God, and remember that God is love. Now which part of this isn't God?"

The little girl shrugged. "I dunno. It's all s'posed to be God, you said."

"That's right." He picked up a larger stone. "So this must be love, because God is love. Right, Maryann?"

She nodded.

"And this is love too, right?" He held up a small pebble and waited for Amy's nod. "Okay, then. If I put this back down here and all this gravel is love, which part of it isn't?"

"It all is." Amy looked pleased with herself.

"If I add this stone, does it change anything?" He picked up a rock from the other side of the sidewalk and tossed it down.

"No, it's still the same."

"And that's exactly how love works. It just keeps growing and growing, no matter how many people you add." He straightened, brushing his hands on his pants.

"You're kind of weird," Amy murmured after a long pause. She motioned for him to bend down. "My mom doesn't like me to say that word."

He nodded. "I know." Clay waved a hand at the parking lot. "There are lots of different stones in there, Amy. But they are still stones, just like God is love no matter how many children He has in His family."

The blue eyes, so like Maryann's studied him for a long time. She cocked her head to one side as she tried to figure it all out.

"Shall we have lunch?" Maryann said finally.

Amy nodded and skipped up the walk to the front door.

"I didn't do that very well, did I?" Clay muttered, his face flushed. "I guess I'm not too used to little kids. I was trying to explain."

"I know." Maryann laid a hand on his arm and smiled. "And you did it very well. She'll think about it for a while and eventually she'll get it."

"My brothers don't come home very often," he told her. "And they never bring their kids. If I want to see 'em, I have to go there. I guess that's why I'm out of practice."

"That's too bad." Maryann found a booth near the back and motioned to it. He followed behind. "Don't they ever want to show the kids where they grew up? See if they have an interest?"

"They don't want anything to do with the farm," he told her, folding himself into the booth. Amy was busy with the menu, so he continued. "They think I'm crazy to pour so much effort into it."

"Why?"

"Oh, I expect they're worried that our dad will come back some day and have some claim on it." He grimaced. "Not very likely after twenty-six years."

Maryann looked up from the menu she was perusing. "Could he do that?" she asked quietly.

Clay raised his eyebrows. "I suppose. Title's never been changed or anything. But if he hasn't shown up by now, I don't think he's going to. For all we know, he could have died years ago."

He shrugged, as if it didn't mean anything to him. But she was alerted by the wistful note in his voice.

"Do you have sweet-and-sour sauce?" Amy demanded of the waitress who'd just shown up. "I'm not having chicken nuggets unless you do."

"Oh, we've got it, honey." The woman smiled. "Lots of it."

"Okay, I'll have them."

They ordered, ate their food with Amy explaining to Clay the proper way to dip a nugget, and then left the restaurant. Ten minutes later Clay turned into a lane overarched with a lacy covering of brilliant green maples.

"You never came out here much, did you?" Clay asked as she stared at the beauty of a farm in full bloom. "I guess we never had many people out in those days. Mom didn't seem to have much time for entertaining."

"It's a lovely site. I've never seen so many flowers." Maryann climbed out of the truck and walked over to the nearest bed of blooming red. "They're beautiful."

"They're perennial," he explained with a shrug. "I just clean them up in the fall, put on some mulch, and take it off again when it warms up. They show up every time."

"Horses!"

Maryann turned to find her daughter transfixed by the sight of two perfectly matched golden palominos standing in the paddock, calmly munching on grass.

"Can I touch them?" Amy's hushed reverent voice brought a smile to Maryann's lips. There wasn't a lot that could cause this kind of wonder in her daughter.

"Do you like horses?" Clay peered down at the little girl, obviously wondering where she'd come in contact with them.

"I don't know. I never had none. Can I pet them?"

"Never had *any*," Maryann reminded. "Clay, can she go nearer?"

"Sure. Just a minute, I'll get Amos. Andy will follow behind. He always does." He stepped between the bar, his voice calm and reassuring as he patted one golden rump. The horse nibbled at his shirt pocket, obviously searching for a treat.

"He's eating you," Amy squealed in delight.

"Naw. He's just looking for this." Clay held out a sugar lump in the middle of his palm. The horse bent his head and regally took the sugar with his teeth.

"Will he bite?" Amy stepped nearer to Clay, her hand sliding into his.

"My horses don't bite," he informed her proudly. "Would you like to try?"

She nodded slowly, her eyes huge as saucers.

"Yes, I would. Please."

Maryann felt her heart rush into her mouth as he lifted her daughter over the rail, placed a sugar cube in the center of her hand, and directed Amy to hold it up.

"Stand very still so he knows you're not teasing him. He'll pick it right up."

She froze, her arm outstretched, as the horse swung his head around and observed the little girl with his placid brown eyes. Then he whinnied softly. Amy stayed put, her lips pressed tightly together. After a moment, the horse ducked his head, brushed his mouth across her palm, and swung it back up.

"Good girl, Amy." Clay laughed and pet the horses's powerful neck. "If you stay still a minute, Andy will come over, then you can give him one too."

"He should have two lumps," Amy whispered, her eyes never leaving the horses. "That other one did."

"Quite right. Here you are, then." He set the two lumps carefully in her hand.

With no apparent fear, Amy held out one hand, the other scrunching her hat back on top of her head. "C'mon horsey. I've got a little treat for you."

Maryann watched the entire event with mixed feelings. It was clear that while Clay might feel he didn't know much about children, he knew exactly how to handle children with animals. The sugar gone, Amy was busy patting the horse's back, her fingers clenched in the tarnished golden mane while her other hand hooked itself around Clay's neck.

He was a natural, Maryann thought. So tender, caring. He made sure she was in no danger, but let her explore the texture of the horse's hair for herself.

"It feels funny, Mommy. And it's so long. You could braid it like you used to do yours." Amy's big grin held not a trace of the sulks. "You know, before Daddy said you looked like a little girl."

Maryann nodded, knowing her cheeks were red, but ignoring it.

"Can I ride this horsey?" Amy asked Clay.

"Not by yourself. But if your mom has time, I could take you for a ride." He glanced at Maryann to see if she approved. "Your mom could come along with us."

"My mom doesn't know how to ride a horse." Amy chuckled at the very idea of it, her eyes sparkling as Clay set her down.

"She used to. Once. A long time ago."

Maryann closed her eyes, remembering the fun of riding one of Clay's horse's as she'd raced across the glen whenever life at her house got too much.

Why couldn't she go back to that time, back to when all she wanted out of life was a secure home and a few new dresses? Why did life have to be so complicated?

You made it that way, her conscience reminded her. *You wanted more and more and more. When will you have enough?*

The question haunted her. Was there enough money in the world to make her feel secure?

"Which one did you ride, Mommy?" Amy tugged on Maryann's slacks, her eyes wide with astonishment.

"A big bay called Flicker. She was as gentle as could be, but could she ever run! She was Clay's horse."

"Really? And Daddy let you?" Clearly the idea was beyond Amy's comprehension.

"I wasn't married then, sweetheart. I was just a girl, a little older than you."

Clay watched as the memories seemed to overwhelm Maryann. He'd been hoping for this when he'd brought her out here. Somehow he'd make her see that this could be her home, that she didn't have to run away again.

"Would you like to ride Andy? He's very gentle and he won't roam far." He kept his voice even, not wanting to frighten her. Don't push, he reminded himself. Let her experience it for herself.

"I'm not wearing the right clothes. Besides, I have to get back to work." She avoided his eyes, bending to pluck a blade of grass that she sliced with her perfectly painted fingernail.

"Do you mind if I take Amy for a ride, then? I promise, she'll be safe."

"Can I, Mommy? Please? Pretty please with sugar and cinnamon on it?"

Maryann grinned at the familiar plea. "You'll have to mind Clay. Do everything he tells you to. Horses need to get used to you, just like friends. They'll be scared if you yell at them."

Amy nodded, eyes huge in her round face. "I will," she whispered.

Clay took the little hand in his and led Amy to the barn, hoping Maryann would follow. When he glanced around, she was there, her hand on the smooth saddle he'd owned for years.

"You still have it," she murmured.

"Yes. I couldn't trade in all the memories." He remembered teaching her how to ride, laughing when she lost her stirrups, picking her up when Flicker had decided a tumble was in order.

He'd taught her to go with the steady gait of the horse, to sit properly, to take a jump. Now he would teach her daughter, God willing.

It took him very little time to saddle the horse, and he swung up easily.

"Okay, Amy. You reach up, and I'll pull you up in front of me. Then we'll let Amos get used to you." He kept his focus on her despite Maryann's distracting presence. "Are you ready?"

"You won't let me drop?" she whispered, fear showing for just a moment.

"No way. And we won't go for long. Okay?"

Amy finally nodded and reached up an arm. Maryann went to lift her, but he shook his head, pulling the child upward.

"That's a girl. Okay, are you comfortable?"

"No. Kinda. I don't know." Amy squirmed a little. When Amos shifted, she stiffened. "Is he mad?"

Clay laughed. "No. He's just getting used to you. Ready?"

She nodded.

"Good girl. Now this is how we get the horse started." He showed her, clicking his teeth just a bit as he jiggled the reins.

"I can't make that noise," Amy told him on a rush of breath. "I don't have my front teeth."

"I noticed that. You better cut down on the sugar lumps." He breathed a sigh of relief when she relaxed and laughed. "Now we're just going to walk a little. Just around the paddock. Do you see Andy following us?" He held her carefully, amazed at the substantial weight of this fragile-looking child in his arms.

Maryann's daughter. She was so tiny and yet so perfect. She wasn't the least bit afraid. He felt an unreasoning pride in her, as if she were his own child.

"Hi, Mommy," Amy called, and then gasped as Amos's head jerked up, his nostrils flaring. She recovered immediately, leaning forward to pat his neck. "It's okay, horsey. I didn't mean to scare you. I won't yell anymore."

The horse snickered softly, tossed his head and continued, obviously reassured. Clay grinned to himself. She certainly was Maryann's child. Amy had the same ability to calm the horse with a few spoken words as her mother had all those years ago.

They walked round the paddock several times until Clay felt he could let the horse canter. Amy seemed to love that, her ringlets tossing in the breeze when she took off her hat.

What would it be like to have a dainty little daughter like this? To watch her grow up, gaining knowledge day by day?

"He's going back to the barn, Mr. Matthews. How come?"

"I guess he's had enough for today. Or maybe he thinks you have." Clay tried to cover his own error of giving the horse his head. "That's all the riding for now, Amy."

"I don't want..." She watched the horse's head jerk up and immediately modulated her voice. "I don't want to stop right now. I'm having so much fun."

"It is fun, isn't it?" Maryann lifted the little girl off and hugged her close. "And it was very nice of Clay to let you ride Amos. Have you thanked him?"

Clay dismounted, watching carefully as Amy walked to the front of the horse, her face bright with interest as she stretched up to pet the graceful neck.

"Thank you very much, Amos. I had a lovely ride."

"Amy, I meant for you to thank Clay!"

Clay burst out laughing at Maryann's dismayed look. "It's all right," he chuckled.

"Thank you very much for the nice ride," she murmured dutifully. The effect was lost in her next words. "When can I ride all by myself?"

"Amy!" Maryann gasped aloud, and Clay recognized the fear in her eyes. "You must never ride these horses alone. Do you understand?"

He laid a hand on Maryann's arm, willing her to look at him. When she did, Clay smiled, his grip tightening just a bit, trying to reassure her. Finally she nodded.

Clay knelt down to Amy's level. "Amy, honey, these horses are too strong for you to manage," he said. "And I don't allow anyone near them unless I'm here. It's dangerous. I promise that I'll take you for another ride the next time your mom brings you out here. That is, if you still want to come," he added slyly.

"Thank you!" She flung her arms around his neck and hugged for all she was worth, only letting go when she finally realized what she was doing. "Oh."

Clay turned away to unsaddle Amos, fully aware that Amy had just realized she'd been fraternizing with the enemy. He didn't understand why she'd put him in that position, but he was determined to change things, even if he had to bribe her with his horse.

"My mom goes to work now," Amy told him, her hat now more on the back of her head than the front. "We might come sometime, though."

"Whenever you like. Maybe I can talk old Molly into letting you have a ride. She usually likes little girls." He sent Amos back into the paddock with a slap on the rump, then turned to Maryann. "I'll show you my workroom now, if you're still interested."

"I certainly am." She nodded and preceded him out

of the barn, her quick glances telling him that she probably remembered his teenage complaints about having to clean the place.

"I have a hired hand now," he told her grinning. "I let him do most of the mucking out."

Clay led her to the shop, feeling a burst of pride at the glistening white building. Once he'd got the place back on its feet, the first thing he'd done was paint every single building. He was determined that his farm would never look rundown again.

"This half is to work on the machinery and stuff," he explained, leading her past the combine that he was overhauling yet again. "Come through here." He opened the door wide, motioned them through and then waited.

"Oh, Clay! This is beautiful!" Maryann ran her fingers down the accordion surface of the rolltop desk he'd made for Ernie Simpson's seventieth birthday. "It's so intricate."

"I like work like that. It makes it worthwhile to have a few secret cubbyholes." He showed off the inside.

"What's this?" Amy was hunkered down in front of a wooden train set he'd just finished. "Is it for somebody?"

"Uh-huh. A mother ordered it for her little boy for Christmas. I've been working on it at night to make sure I had it finished. I wouldn't want to disappoint him."

"This dining room suite will be gorgeous." Maryann turned to him, her eyes full of wonder. "Everything is so smooth, so carefully done. There's not a rough edge anywhere. You do lovely work."

"Thank you." He felt his chest puff up with pride.

"It's no wonder you want to go into business. People must flock to you." She fingered the partly finished wall unit he was making for Caitlin. "She's going to love this. It glows like honey."

"The business will be nip and tuck for a while. I'll use the farm as backup for those times when business drops a bit. The income from it will keep me afloat. But eventually I'd like to work at it full time. There's something satisfying in this that I don't always find in farming."

"I can imagine." She sat on one of several breakfast bar stools. "These swivel!"

"They're for the pastor's kitchen." He nodded, pleased that she appreciated them. But then, Maryann was an artist herself. She loved the play of light and color, and her pictures were vignettes of life at its peak.

"Anyway, that's my idea." He checked to be sure Amy wasn't too close to overhear. "So you see, you wouldn't have to be a farm wife if you married me. If everything goes well, I should be a full-time carpenter by next spring."

"Clay, I don't have anything against farms. Well, not so much anymore," she revised as she saw his raised brow. "But I really don't think it's a good idea for me to talk about this just now. I need time to let the past go, to help Amy deal with her new life here in Oakburn."

"And you can't do that with me in the picture? I'd like to help Amy too." He wondered what brought that shadow to Maryann's face. A quick glance around the room satisfied him that Amy was busy looking at the rest of his creations. Thankfully, she was too far away to hear them.

"Clay, it's not that I don't think you'd be a wonderful father. I'm sure you would. You're kind and caring with children, and they respond to that."

He saw her hands twist together and knew she was trying to tell him something. But what? Everything inside urged him to find out what it was, to demand she say yes. But as he glimpsed the wash of emotion in her eyes, he held back, waiting, hoping she'd trust him enough to explain.

"It's me, you see. I'm not at all the person I was ten years ago."

"So, who is?"

"You are. Don't you see? You want the same things—a home, a family, a wife—"

"I want you," he added, but he didn't think she'd heard.

"I want those things too, but I can't just fly into another relationship. Not yet. I have to think it through, be sure of things, weigh the pros and cons."

"What you mean is that you're not sure that I can give you all the things he could. Isn't that right?" He turned away, hands stiff at his sides. "Well, you're right, sweetheart. I don't have a big penthouse, or a fancy car, or enough money in my back pocket to pay for half a dozen trips a year."

"That isn't—"

"Isn't it? Isn't that exactly what you've always wanted, Maryann? I thought—no *hoped*—that by now you'd see that life is more than things, more than the sum total of someone's assets. But I guess not."

Defeat nagged at him, sucking away the pleasure he'd felt only moments ago.

"You must have plenty of money by now. By all accounts, your husband left you fairly well off. Why do you need more? When will it be enough, Mary-ann?''

''Oh!''

He turned back at the sound and realized she was angry. Red spots of color dotted her pale skin; her black hair seemed to spark as it swirled around her.

''Don't you make me out to be a gold digger, Clay Matthews!'' She stood in front of him, full of temper, blue eyes flashing like lightning. ''I'm not, and you know it.''

''Do I?'' he muttered softly, feeling guilty for condemning her.

''You should. Yes, I like nice clothes, paying the rent, knowing I have a bank balance that isn't in the red. What's wrong with that?'' She glared at him defiantly.

''Nothing.''

''You're right! It's something I didn't grow up with, you can be sure of that. We never knew from one month to the next if we'd have to move, or if there'd be enough to put food on the table. I wore more hand-me-downs than I want to think about. I need security in my life. That's who I am, Clay. Not some perfect dream woman you've concocted in your mind.''

Clayton stepped backward, shocked at the fury in the slim, graceful figure.

''Planning things, getting life in order, knowing where you are and what's going to happen to you is important to me. I spent too many years wondering if my brothers and sisters were going to be taken away. I saw too many social workers come and take notes about the shack we lived in to feel comfortable living hand to mouth.''

''Maryann, I'm not asking you to do that,'' he

gasped, unable to believe that he hadn't known things were so bad in her home. Why hadn't she ever let on? "But life doesn't always come with ironclad guarantees for security. All we know is that God is in control."

"What happens if your business fails?" she countered. One slim hand encompassed all his painstaking work. "This is a farming community. If the crops don't come off, people don't buy. What happens to your furniture then?"

"Don't worry, we wouldn't starve."

"How can I know that? How can I be sure my daughter won't suffer for my decision?"

He considered telling her about the nest egg he'd socked away to ensure that his business wouldn't end up in the hole. But something in him backed away from that. Some voice whispered that he might regret it down the road.

Would Maryann marry him if she thought he had money?

He didn't want that, Clay realized sadly. He didn't want her love when it was couched in and protected by money. He wanted her to love him because of who he was. He wanted her to come to him, to love him, without any guarantee but that he loved her too. He wanted her to trust him to provide for her and Amy. He wanted her to show some faith in him.

It was probably too much to ask.

"I'd better take you home. It's getting late," he said finally.

It wasn't, but that didn't matter. Nothing did, except the fact that Maryann MacGregor didn't believe in him any more now than she had ten years ago. It was a bitter pill to swallow.

"I'm sorry, Clay. But I need time. I need to think, consider everything very carefully before I take such a major step." She moved closer, her hand lifting to cup his cheek. "I do care for you, Clay. But can't we just be friends for now? Please don't push this." Her voice rose, drawing her daughter's attention.

"I want to go home." Amy pushed her way between them, her glance chilly when it touched Clay. "Mommy?"

"Yes, sweetie. Clay is just taking us. Did you like the things he made?"

"I guess." She stood considering Clay, her face wrinkled up in a frown. "Mr. Matthews, can I ask you somethin'?"

"Sure, Amy." He hunched down in front of her. "But call me Clay, okay?" she nodded. "What is it?"

"It's not here," she said. "I have to show you."

"Okay." Puzzled, Clay followed her through the workshop to the far door. His heart dropped as he realized where she was heading.

"What's this?" Amy pointed at his latest project—the one he'd sunk heart and soul into during every spare moment he could find.

"It's going to be a sleigh." He saw Maryann's eyes widen as she took in the big wooden frame with its curling scrollwork. Her eyes flashed a question.

"For Santa?" the little girl demanded.

"No, for your mom and me." He bent down again, so that his eyes were level with Amy's. Maybe the only way he could get to Maryann was through her daughter. "Do you remember I told you I had a secret memory?"

The little girl nodded, her face solemn. "Uh-huh."

"Well, this sleigh is part of my memory."

"It can't be," she argued, her forehead wrinkling. "This is new—not old like memories."

"That's true. Will you listen for a minute, while I tell you a story?" She nodded doubtfully. "Okay, then." He heard Maryann draw closer but concentrated his attention on Amy.

"I have one very special memory of a long time ago. I don't think I was as big as you, but I'm not sure. Not all of it is really clear. But what I do remember is that one night when it was winter and really cold outside, my dad took me for a sleigh ride. He hooked up the horses to pull the sleigh, put bells on their harnesses, and then he piled us boys into that sleigh."

Clay closed his eyes, reliving every detail in his mind. "We went up and down the hills, giggling and laughing, sticking out our tongues so the snow from the branches we hit would fall on us."

"'Laughing all the way,'" Amy whispered, her mouth smiling. "I know that song."

"Yes," he agreed softly. "'Laughing all the way.' It seemed like a long, long time that I rode in the sleigh, snuggled up on my dad's lap. I was the littlest, you see, and it felt so nice to be held close like that."

"Did you only go once?" she asked, her little face glowing with curiosity.

"Yes. Just once. My dad sold the sleigh to someone else. After that, I never saw either him or the sleigh again."

"Did he die too?" One small hand came up to caress his cheek tenderly, imparting her sympathy for that small boy.

He shook his head. "I don't think so. But I don't know for sure. He just never came back home."

"Why?"

"I don't know, Amy. I don't know."

"Daddies shouldn't go away," she said quietly. "They should stay with their fam'lies." Amy seemed deep in thought as she stroked one tiny fingernail along the intricate pattern he'd carved into the side panel.

"I guess you want to ride with your little boy in a sleigh, don't you?" she guessed finally.

"I want to ride with your mom in this sleigh someday."

He shouldn't have said it out loud. Amy jumped back from the wood as if her hand had been burned. She moved to her mother's side and thrust her hands up, mutely asking to be held.

He held her gaze, his own steady as he told her the truth that burned inside. "I want to marry your mom, Amy. I'd like to have you and her as part of my family. One day, after we get married, I want us to ride in that sleigh together as a family."

Silence—drawn out, painful, full of questions. Maryann threw him an angry look before glancing down at her daughter. Amy stood where she was, but she stamped her foot in temper.

"No!" she yelled. "You can't marry my mom. She doesn't even like you. And neither do I. You're not our fam'ly." She turned, tugging Maryann's hand as she searched for the way out. "I'm not coming back to ride your silly old horses ever."

Clay followed them back through the shop and out into the late-afternoon sunshine. He wasn't surprised to see tears on Amy's cheeks, and he called himself a fool for sharing his dream. It wasn't the right time. He should have kept it to himself a little longer.

"I'll take you home," he told Maryann quietly.

She nodded. "I think that would be best."

"And we're not ever coming back here, are we, Mommy? Are we?"

Amy's insistent cries tugged at Clay's heart. He longed to take her in his arms, to reassure her that he would always take care of both of them.

But as the child clung to her mother and ignored his overtures, he realized how futile it was.

There was nothing he could say to make it better for Amy. Nothing at all. Maybe it was better to just leave the two of them alone for a while, and let God handle the rest.

Chapter Seven

Maryann glanced around the big hall surreptitiously, trying to find him. Clay had to be here somewhere, because he'd told Jordan he was coming to the Oakburn annual 4H July masquerade and square dance.

"Looking for someone?" Beth poked her head out from the fishing pond she was arranging. "Like a certain Mr. Matthews, perhaps?"

"Just looking around. You know, checking who's here. That kind of thing." Maryann pretended nonchalance.

"Uh-huh!" Beth's impish grin was infectious. "And I'm Mary, Queen of Scots."

"Really?" Maryann gave her the once-over. "You look more like a serf." She burst into laughter at Beth's grimace.

"It's this stupid costume. I was trying to make an elf costume in the hope that my dear sister would consent to wear it for our Christmas open house." She tugged at her pointed, felt-green skirt with bells attached. "Something tells me my sewing is a bit rusty."

"You look great. I was just teasing. Anyway, *I* should talk." Maryann glanced down at her own orange balloons. "This looked so easy in the magazine."

"It's actually very good. Pumpkins are all the rage this year. Besides, another few weeks and it will be autumn." Beth's eyes lit up and she snickered. "The Lone Ranger just walked in. I assume he left Silver outside. Aren't you going over to say 'hi'?"

"The Lone...oh." Maryann swallowed hard when she caught sight of Clayton's outfit.

He was covered in black from head to foot. On the heels of his boots he wore silver spurs. On his hips twin holsters with toy guns sat waiting. As she watched, he whipped one out and squirted it at Jordan, aiming for and hitting his mouth with a steady stream of water. The group of men surrounding him burst into laughter.

She would have known Clay anywhere, in spite of the black eye mask. His Stetson sat tilted at the same rakish angle, one lock of hair curling against his left eyebrow. On his chest he wore a big silver star.

Her heart tripped double time as he strode across the room toward her. "Howdy, ma'am."

"Howdy, yourself. Nice outfit. Do I call you 'Lone' for short?" She couldn't help it—laughter bubbled out at his abashed face.

"I didn't think you'd recognize me," he mumbled, shoving his hands in his pockets. "I haven't seen you for a while. How are you?"

"I'm fine. And you?"

"Okay. I was hoping you and Amy might come out